Wild Words

Volume 2

Leitrim County Council Arts Office,
Aras an Chontae,
Carrick on Shannon,
Co. Leitrim,
Ireland.

00353 7196 21694

www.leitrimarts.ie

ISBN: 9780957618923

Edited by Helen Carr

A collection of writing by young people produced in association with the Wild Words Children's Literature Festival, Carrick on Shannon, Leitrim.

Published by Leitrim County Council Arts Office

Foreword

This is the second year that Leitrim County Council has put out a call for writing submissions from teenagers for inclusion in *Wild Words* and, as with *Volume 1*, we were amazed at the quantity and quality of submissions from all across Ireland. I was delighted to be asked to return as the editor of *Wild Words, Volume 2*. I was so impressed by all the entries, encouraged to see how many young people are interested in writing and amazed by the breadth of subjects and narrative styles explored in their writing. It was difficult to narrow all the submissions down to the twenty-seven that made up the final selection, but it had to be done.

Once again, what I strove to include in this collection were strong storylines and ideas, credible characters and high-quality writing; I think all the stories in *Wild Words, Volume 2* fulfill these criteria.

During the teenage years, interests broaden, young people begin to move beyond the family circle, develop their own opinions and views, and hone their skills in their own areas of interest – I think that growth is very apparent in this collection. Some themes can be seen across many of the entries as the young writers explore issues that reflect their reality, look back to childhood or ahead to adulthood. Also, I often spotted the influence of current trends in literature and other art forms as the writers explore different genres and voices; good writers are often avid readers too.

There's a lot of darkness in this collection; some of the pieces use writing to explore more difficult topics – whether imagined ones like dystopian worlds, dark forces in fantasy worlds, or the more topical darkness of the modern world like war and terrorism. Some of the stories reflect the zeitgeist of many current art forms – books, television drama and films – by having an anti-hero protagonist who takes us inside the mind of what would be considered evil or disturbed characters. But there are also stories looking honestly at teen life as it is lived today – feelings about school, the pain of not fitting in or being bullied, the excitement of flirting, staying out late, pushing the boundaries or finding romance.

This honest, varied collection, showcases the vibrancy and variety of our young writers. Read and enjoy!

Helen Carr

August 2014

Helen Carr has worked in publishing for seventeen years and is a senior editor with The O'Brien Press. She has worked with many Irish children's authors including Judi Curtin, Oisín McGann, Celine Kiernan, Alan Nolan, Ruth Francis Long, Chris Judge and Sheila Agnew. Helen has also reviewed children's books for many publications including The Sunday Independent, Inis magazine and BookFest.

Contents

The Silence After A Gunshot

By Ryan Finnegan, aged 15

My mouth was dry and my heart beat so hard I thought it would burst from my chest. I looked at her with rage and disgust. The never-ending song began as usual. That night is one I try and try to forget, but as long as I hear that song, as long as I can imagine that song taking me over, I never will forget what happened. You have to understand that it's not my fault. You must realise it's that song.

But anyway, hello! My name is Stephen Brown, I'm 38 years old and I'm married (well sort of, but I'll come to that later on). For now I want to tell you why it's that song's fault, not mine, which in turn, I guess, will explain why I'm 'sort of' married. Great. I'll kill two birds with one stone.

As I approached my home earlier than usual (because I may possibly have gotten fired), I noticed a car in my parking space. This was strange, as no one ever seemed to visit ever since... But it is in no way necessary to dwell on so small a distraction. I warily parked my car on the road outside my house. I walked in the door 'Honey, I'm home!' I shouted up the stairs, anxiously waiting for my wife to attack me over why I was home so early. (I get fired a lot). I heard scrambling and shout-whispers above me. 'Not again, please not again.' Then the song began.

I ran upstairs and suddenly was confronted by a half-naked guy jumping out a window into the rose bush beneath him outside. The song got louder. I screamed, louder than I possibly imagined I ever could. I jumped down the stairs two at a time and ran over to the half-naked guy. I heard my terrified wife pleading with me to stop hitting him. How could I? I hit him and hit him and hit him until it became so monotonous that I almost become a machine brutally beating the guy. My wife was now behind me 'Stop, stop, Jack ST—' I keep hitting him. I don't know how many times I hit

1

him; just couldn't concentrate, not with that song blaring in my head. Anyway, you get the picture, the guy died.

Sorry, I know, they really think I should ease into that part of the story but I can't, the only thing I remember after that is the song, our wedding song: 'AND I... Will Always Love You.' Do you understand that it's not my fault? These little outbursts I have, it's that song. Now, some people say I'm a full blown psychopath, which is actually very funny because if you asked anyone who actually knows me they'd disagree, excluding the people who say that about me, obviously.

I am still sort of married though. My wife didn't file for the divorce. However she did get a restraining order. That's good though, right? A restraining order is temporary and our love is infinite. She must still love me. I know she does. She must.

Some things I didn't mention above:

1. I didn't have a job in the first place, I was coming home from an AA meeting
2. 34 times, I do remember
3. The reason why my wife stopped saying 'Stop' was because I had turned around and slapped her, my biggest regret
4. My wife wasn't cheating on me
5. The guy wasn't even half naked
6. The guy was fixing tiles on my roof and simply fell
7. My wife did file for divorce

Something else I didn't mention in the 'things I didn't mention above', above

1. I was actually coming home from the pub, pfft ... AA meeting.

The reason why people never visited me, and why I had thought 'not again' when I thought my wife was cheating on me, was because this hadn't been my first outburst. My first outburst was for the same reason, actually. It happened a year after I had married my wife. We were expecting our first child at that time and we needed more space than my crammed little apartment. We moved to this huge house just down the road. The house had a homely feel to it, almost as if we had lived there for years. We loved it. After two weeks of settling in, I started to notice how often the local carpenter was coming to 'varnish the floor'. I became suspicious. How long does it take to varnish a floor? When I questioned him he came up with pathetic excuses 'The floor needed to be re-stripped.' The song began. 'I needed to put on a second coat'. The excuses kept coming until all I heard was the song building up with verses and the bridge until finally the chorus began with my fist and his jaw.

The song stopped. I became flustered and then the drums came, a build-up making my heart race until the chorus came back stronger than ever. I repeated the chorus until my wife pulled me off the carpenter. I fell back onto her, and being on the heavy side, I crushed her. She screeched and I hurried to my feet to help her up. It was then that the song was replaced with a gut wrenching thought – 'the baby'. There and then I had just murdered my baby... And it was the carpenter's fault. I turned and shouted louder and more vicious than ever 'YOU!' I stared right into the carpenter's eyes as the song chorus came back with a twist. The twist being my foot. I kicked him and boxed him until I was sure he was dead and the song had come to a close. I would do anything for the song to stop, for that awful night to stop recurring in my head.

Some things I didn't mention above, again... Sorry

1. This wasn't my first outburst.
2. My first outburst was the reason we moved. I had started a fire in the apartment because I believed that my wife was cheating on me with a guy who was sorting out the pipes in the bathroom, and the only way to get him to come out was to start the fire. The song's fault again.

I don't just have outbursts like these when I am suspicious of my wife. I remember being in a supermarket two months after my wife's fatal 'miscarriage'. It had been two months since I had been out of the house. Everyone was looking at me. I didn't need to check, I just knew. I knew people would glance at me, look away and then two seconds later realise whom they had just seen. That doesn't annoy me or irritate me in any way, if anything I feel a little famous. All I had to do was get some milk. But they just had to, didn't they? I approached the milk fridge, head down, and then I heard 'This is an oldie for all you love birds out there' on the supermarket speakers. Before I knew it, the song had begun. Why? Why put on a radio in a supermarket? I tried to ignore it. I was unsuccessful. At first I did what my doctor told me which was to try and get out of the situation and calm down. Easier said than done. Try explaining to a security guard that you're running out of a shop like a lunatic because you hate the song that's playing. Hate is actually too mild to describe how it makes me feel. So I went to ground with my hands crushing my ears, curled up in a ball screaming, in the middle of one of the aisles. The security guard came over to me and got in my face telling me to 'Shut Up' and to 'Get out'. I screamed so loudly and then I couldn't control it. I hit him and hit him until he sprayed my eyes with pepper spray, which was a lot more painful than I had ever imagined. That day was the worst day of my life. It was worse than killing those guys. I didn't even get my milk.

Some things I didn't mention above:

1. The song was actually in my heads, not on the radio
2. I never even tried to control my outburst, I couldn't
3. The security guard wasn't even in my face, he was actually nice, helping me outside

A question a lot of people ask me is, 'Why your wedding song?' The answer is simply that I caught my wife having an affair with another man with our wedding song blaring from the CD player beside them. And when I say caught, I mean caught, walked in, however you want to say it. At first all I could do was laugh. Until the guy turned to me and said 'You should probably leave'. The laughing stopped and I boiled. 'To our wedding song? Really?' I said to my wife almost in tears. She looked at me with confusion and sorrow. 'Stephen, he's right, you should go.' Is it just me or am I the only one who thinks I had the right to shoot that guy in the face? Which is what I did. I pulled out my handgun from the sock drawer and shot the guy.

The silence after a gunshot is one like no other silence. My mouth was dry and my heartbeat so hard I thought it would burst from my chest, I looked at her with rage and disgust. I walked casually to her, stepping over the guy's body as if it were no big deal, I looked at her in the eye and said, 'I came in, you shouted rape and I'll be a hero'. Still shocked by what just happened, her mouth gawking open at the pool of blood, she wouldn't look at me. 'Call 999, and you tell them what I told you. He came in he grabbed you yada, yad,a yada, my husband came in and shot him, saved the day, you fill in the details.'

So what's happening with me now? Well as you know, my wife filed for a restraining order and divorced me, but in fairness she hasn't blabbed about me being a murderer. You see she must understand that anyone I kill, well, it's her fault. Her fault for picking our wedding song. Her fault for committing adultery while it played. Her fault. Not mine.

Some things that were never mentioned above:

1. My ex-wife's name is Annie
2. I am a compulsive liar, you've probably realised
3. It's not the songs fault
4. I am a full-blown psychopath.

Home

by Naoise Cunningham, aged 14

There's a boy standing at the window, watching the rain fall heavy on the glass-plated window, a portal into the outside world. He watches the lush green grass; he sees the purity of the objects as the water seemingly washes away their sins. He hears the patter of the rain, the chirping of the midday songbird as it whistles its merry business. He can smell the wet, plant-like odour of the beating rain; almost taste its slight acidity. Yet all these senses are but secondary to the thought that preoccupies his mind. This is a thought that all eight-year-olds think of at one stage or another, a great fantasy of youth. It is the thought. It is The Thought of Running Away.

He sees himself in the jungle, battling through the tropical heat as the natives creep up on him. He is flying, falling, and then suddenly whisked off again, this time another far away land, where dragons roam freely, and damsels in distress are a-plenty. This is all swirling around an eight-year-old boy's head as he gazes out the window. And then he decides, in a fit of adventure, to go, leave home, rescue a dazzling princess from fierce dragons, battle savage natives in a tropical jungle, live the life of a pirate on board a Jolly Roger flying ship, and do a thousand more things besides.

He races upstairs to his bedroom and grabs his old school bag, his very own rucksack, and gathers provisions for his journey. He obtains a pack of crackers from the pantry, locates an old orange skulking at the bottom of the rucksack and a soggy packet of almost edible biscuits is found lurking behind the couch. He then prepares for the arduous journey that lies ahead of him, a journey of mystery and magic, one in which fantasy is inexplicably intertwined with reality. He sets off down the stairs and creeps past the kitchen door. The singing that usually emanates from there now sounds like a native war cry. Cautiously he creeps to the Fort of Cushions and smites the mighty dragon as he stands. As he stands there, basking in the dead dragon's reflective golden scales, he reflects himself. What will I be like in nine years' time, he muses? Will I still be rescuing beautiful princesses, and defending myself from evil, savage, wild tribes, he wonders. Or perhaps I will be their leader, their overlord, leading an idyllic lifestyle. Or will I run off, strike out on my own? What will I be like, he ponders? And then the Great All-Powerful Voice rang out.

'Dinner's ready!'

And off he ran.

***

There is a boy standing at the window, watching the rain fall heavy on the glass-plated window, a portal into the outside world. He is almost a man, but still not legally accepted by society, a reject from the adult-only conferences. He watches the world passing by, the blur of the cars as they pass by in the now beating rain. He sits and watches it silently, as he knows this may be his last view of the house opposite him, the last view of the sparrow's nest in front of his window. He watches the world pass by with a sort of melancholy feeling in his heart. Yet as he thinks of this, of the journey, the adventure ahead of him, he sits up a little straighter, his pulse quickens. That small drop of sadness in his heart melts away, replaced with a vision of exploration, a voyage through unexplored territories. He sets down his box of keepsakes, and walks over to the window. An almost long-forgotten memory stirs inside, threatening to spill over from the depths of a neglected corner of his brain. But he quickly brushes it aside.

Off he goes, down the stairs, on what is a small journey, but can't possibly be, a step away from the boy he once was, to a man with a new adventure ahead of him.

He grazes against the banister, his fingers lingering on the wall. A sadness takes hold of him once more, however this one has a slightly more melancholy feel to it. He thinks about the adventures he used to have, of times spent, gone in a whirlwind of years. He thinks of how much he has progressed since then, his first day of school, his first teacher, his first holiday, his first argument, his first girlfriend, his first kiss. These things all seem irrelevant, pointless to some distant observer. And yet they are the most important, defining things in his life. He remembers all these memories, and more, while that hand lingers on the flaking wall. A time well spent, was it, or a time neither here nor there in the course of what we call human history?

He picks up the last stray books that lie on the bed. The last pencil is thrown away. And as he does this a sense of excitement comes upon him. The pace that he works at clearing out his room, the desk, the knick-knacks hardly contain his eagerness to leave home, to set out on his expedition of voyage and discovery. He works for several hours with unadulterated zeal, until a voice calls out, 'Dinner's ready!'

And with that voice a memory goes off in his head like a gunshot. He creeps past the kitchen, a singing voice emanates from there, now cracked with age. He walks past the couch, with its new upholstery, lacking the cushions to build a fort that he once loved to do. He sees the dragons in his mind's eye, swooping around, trying to capture the princess, to whom he has sworn his life. Then he is in the jungle, the natives' cries screaming from the treetops, him sweating from the tropical weather. And then all of a sudden he is back in the present; he is twirling around an empty sitting room, a portrait of a man staring back at him. He gently sets the makeshift sword down, and gazes solemnly at the picture. It is cracked and slightly musty with age, but still commands a graceful type of authority, a type of respect. Slowly one tear trickles down the side of his face but he keeps his stare steady. He slowly walks out of the room, his gusto gone, deflated. And he swiftly runs into the kitchen.

'Oh, there you are, love. I was getting worried about you.'

This is received with a large embrace of pure love, and of thanks for all the years spent minding him. He sobs quietly, 'I don't want to go.'

And is met with an even bigger hug.

'Of course you do, silly. You do because I know you do, and sometimes I know you better than you do.'

And with that a tingly feeling spreads through his body, one of warmth spreads from his fingers to his toes. It traverses along every inch of his form. And with that hug, that one act of kindness, love and comfort, that eagerness to face the next big adventure returns. The forgotten memory is reborn. He remembers what it is like to want to run away, that eagerness to leave home. And he remembers that he wondered what it would be like to leave home at seventeen. And at that moment he remembered that he was ready. He was ready to leave home.

Human

by Phoebe Lawlor, aged 14

It started with a car crash. Fourteen-year-old Abigail Maison sat in the back seat of her parents' car, arguing with them. They were talking about moving again. She hated moving so much and it was so unfair that she kept having to leave her friends. She started shouting at her mother who was driving and shouting back as her father kept telling them to calm down which only made things worse. Her mother turned around to look at Abigail and her father started shouting at his wife to keep her eyes on the road. Abigail sat in the back scowling at them refusing to speak. In the next few moments she'll have wished that she never even opened her mouth.

The truck appeared out of nowhere. It came straight at the car and her parents turned around just in time to see its blinding headlights come crashing into their car. That was the last thing either of them ever saw. Abigail felt a piercing pain as a large shard of glass impaled her. She watched helplessly as her life flashed before her eyes, then she felt nothing .Her surroundings faded away and with it the pain. She was at a standstill. She was in a numb emptiness. And yet she felt relieved her worries and memories started to slip away and just as she was settling into this state of oblivion she heard an ear-piercing scream. Everything came flooding back to her. First her memories, then her surroundings and lastly her pain. The pain was the worst. It hit her full force and she cried out as she tried to stand up. It took her several minutes to actually notice what was around her and when she did she wished she had died. The scene was a mixture of broken glass dented metal and blood. Abigail looked at her parents, their heads lolling to the side their blood mixing with hers in a pool on the car floor. She looked into her mother's lifeless eyes and watched her father's still chest void of breath that had moved it only moments before. Then she cried. She cried and screamed ripping out the shard of glass barely noticing the pain, as it didn't nearly compare to the pain she felt for her parents. The blood gushed out of the open wound but all Abigail felt was emptiness inside like someone had created a black hole inside of her and it was beginning to destroy her from the inside out. With salty tears still dripping down her pale face and mingling with the thick blood on the floor she leaned over to her mother's body, still slightly warm, and kissed her. She did the same to her father, gently kissing his fading red cheek. After pulling herself away she whispered to them in a voice that only they'd hear, 'I love you.' She stumbled out of the car, and without looking back she ran.

She wanted to be as far away from the crash as possible. As if not being able to see it would make it not real. She managed a good mile despite her injury before she dropped to the ground outside a small coffee shop finding it difficult to breathe. Sitting on the cold hard pavement at seven in the morning, before the streets would get busy, Abigail Maison curled up in a ball, squeezed her eyes shut and put her fingers in her ears blocking out all outside sound and pain. She remained there for at least twenty minutes until a waiter inside the coffee shop saw her through the window and called an ambulance. What happened next was all a blur. The guards came and took a statement from the waiter while the paramedics came with a stretcher to bring Abigail to the ambulance. She kicked and screamed and cried, but she didn't feel like she was in her body she felt like she was watching someone else. Eventually she stopped fighting and lay perfectly still, feeling disconnected from reality. She didn't know if they'd found her parents' bodies but she didn't want to think about that, she just wanted to lie there hoping beyond all hope that this was a nightmare and she could wake up and see her parents and live a normal life. But then the pain came back and she knew this was real.

The ambulance brought her to the hospital where she was put into emergency care. She hadn't heard any mention of her parents or the crash and the guards wouldn't be speaking to her until she was better. But she would never be better, that pain that her parents' death left would never go away and her last words to them would haunt her forever 'You're ruining my life,' she wanted

11

to get sick at the thought of that being the last thing they ever heard her say to them. As the afternoon came and went, with the doctors rushing around her, taking out pieces of glass, stopping the bleeding, Abigail began to realise that she should have died. The glass should have killed her. And she knew from looking at the doctors, that they were as confused as her. She kept wondering about this as she was brought in for surgery. She couldn't be put asleep but they used so many drugs to stop the pain that once they kicked in and the surgery began, she was barely able to think of what she had for breakfast that morning. It would have been a blissful relief to not feel the pain or have to worry but it felt forced and there was something trying to claw its way to the front of her mind. Alone in the hospital room that night she realised what it was. Lying under those stuffy hospital sheets she put two and two together. She survived a fatal accident, she managed to run in critical condition, the pain had been terrible but not as bad as it should have been, now she could barely even feel the pain and it had nothing to do with the painkillers and probably the strangest of all, her wound was already practically healed and the stitches were falling out. After thinking through each anomaly that had occurred throughout her whole life Abigail finally realised that she wasn't human.

She was released from hospital three days later and was collected outside the dull grey building by a social care worker. Abigail had no known family apart from her parents so she was taken to the nearest children's home called 'Hope's Academy for children' which was originally a boarding school and was nicknamed 'HAC'. Her social worker's name was Grace McGraw and was one of those people who tried too hard. After half an hour of driving while trying to start conversation Grace sighed and continued the rest of the journey in silence. They pulled up outside a large depressing building, which was painted a dull, cream-brown and had small plain windows. Once Abigail went inside she realised that the building outside only reflected the mood inside. There were children everywhere of varying ages and although many of them were playing or watching TV, none of them seemed particularly happy. A woman named Marian came to take Abigail's bag upstairs and show Abigail her room. Marian owned this 'facility' and seemed kind, but strict, with slightly not enough patience to be working with these kids. She shut the door on her way out and left Abigail alone in a little three-bed room with one set of shelves, a slightly lopsided wardrobe and a dinky wooden desk with a matching chair. The nicest thing in the room was the window on the far wall. It went out a bit so you could sit in it and look out towards the horizon pretending to be somewhere else even just for a moment. She had to share a room with two similar aged kids. A twelve-year-old, down-to-earth girl named Hazel and a fourteen-year-old boy named Lucas. Although Abigail wouldn't speak to most people at the home, she got on particularly well with these two and probably would have gone insane without them especially after her parents' funeral. It was three weeks after arriving at 'HAC' that Abigail received her parents' old stuff. Everything that they left for her came in an old slightly damp cardboard box that smelt of mould, old books and Abigail's old attic. The box contained the usual stuff at the top; a piece of jewellery passed down from generations, a photo album full of family memories, a couple of books ranging from cooking to gardening to novels, her parents' wedding rings, a hat belonging to her father and a scarf belonging to her mother. At the bottom however there was a sealed letter addressed to someone called 'Eloise' in gold writing, another sealed letter with her name hastily written on the back and a beautiful, decorated wooden box about the size of a jewellery box. She took the letter with the gold writing and carefully opened it making sure not to rip anything. It was a very formal letter, although it contained very little writing.

Dear Ms Eloise,

We are most delighted to inform that you have been accepted into 'Hallow Oaks Academy' and will be beginning first thing this September. Further information will be sent throughout the summer by our postage system but should you have any further inquiries feel free to contact us,

Yours most sincerely,

Frederick Down

Abigail stared down at the piece of paper three things going through her mind, who was this Eloise, what is 'Hallow Oaks Academy' and how could she contact them without a phone number or email address? She decided to brush these questions aside and see what the other letter said. She recognised her mother's messy writing.

Dear Abigail,

I don't have much time to explain but what I want you to understand why we did what we did. If you're reading this now then your father and I did not make it and I'm sorry for that but you must know we did everything we could to keep you safe even if we had to give up our own lives. Now that we are gone you must look after yourself and to do so you must understand what I'm about to tell you. Your father and I were part of an organisation called LEP. At first it was just an organisation dedicated to science, but one day that changed. Each department or sector had to swear an oath of lifelong loyalty to the organisation and its 'projects.' We were part of the research department and our job was to research new discoveries made by other departments. It was while researching a new element found off the coast of Mexico that your father accidentally accessed some private files that contained LEP's real intention. They were gathering information to create a substance that could be given to humans to make them into a form of superhuman with faster healing, more strength and better reactions. What they planned to do with these humans is unknown as any human they tested it on died afterwards, as their body couldn't handle it, that is, for all but one. We knew we had to leave the organisation. But once you're part of LEP you aren't allowed to leave. Your father and I escaped but we've been on the run ever since. They want to kill us because we know too much and if you're reading this they probably already have although it will most likely have looked like an accident. There is much more I need to tell you if only I had the time. But this is urgent; you must not let them get you. They will come after you if they know you're alive. That one human who survived the 'superhuman project', that was you. They took you from us and injected you with a high amount of their newest formula and it worked even better than they thought because instead of being superhuman you became inhuman. They wanted to keep you to study and train to become their weapon but we stole you back from them and have been trying to keep you safe. Now they'll want to find you and either research you or kill you. This might all be hard to understand but just know your father and I love you so much.

Much Love,

Your mother and father

P.S. We had to change your name. Your real name is Eloise Thyme and there should be another letter showing that you got accepted into the best top secret fighting school worldwide. We enrolled you at Christmas and you can still go (all expenses are paid).

Abigail's hands shook as she put down the letter. How had she not known about her parents' secret lives on the run while she'd been a part of it? She sat staring at the last item, the wooden box; she hadn't even known her real name. With trembling fingers she gently opened the carved lid to reveal a silver dagger, with diamond along the blade and a beautifully designed handle made out of a deep blue stone and glittering opal gems, lying on a rich purple silk lining. There was a short note that read, 'For your protection'. With love, mom and dad.' She gave herself a moment to breathe then got up went over to her old school bag and began to pack.

She felt bad leaving Hazel and Lucas, but she knew deep down that she had to go. The next night she went to bed fully clothed and waited for everyone to go to sleep. She got up just after midnight after not hearing anyone for about twenty minutes and left a note on the desk to tell Hazel and Lucas that she was ok and she'd miss them. Then she picked up her bag snuck out the door down the hall and out the sitting room window. As she ran silently away from 'HAC' she made a resolution to leave her life as Abigail Maison behind her and begin her life as Eloise Thyme, whose goal was to find 'LEP' and destroy it.

Eloise didn't stop running until she was sure that there was plenty of distance between her and the children's home. She ducked into an old abandoned building to get some rest, knowing that soon they'd be looking for her and she'd have to leave the city. She also knew that she'd need food, water and other supplies to survive. Feeling an unwelcome wave of despair she opened one of her parents' old books to distract herself and hopefully help her dose off. She picked out one of the novels but when she opened it she got the biggest shock. Inside was a section cut out of the book and it held the largest pile of 20 euro notes Eloise had ever seen. Upon opening the remaining books she found that they all contained money some 10s some 20s and some 50s, enough to keep her going until she could find a way to make some money. With this new burst of determination came a burst of energy and so Eloise packed up her books and set off to buy some supplies for her journey ahead. She was in a part of the city that she didn't know and so no one recognised her as she quickly went from shop to shop getting food, water, some rope from a camping shop, a penknife, a disposable phone and a digital watch which displayed time and date. It was then that she realised she'd need new clothes, so she bought a fitted black tank top, a grey hoodie, a pair of leggings and a pair of black sneakers. She bought some make-up, a sunhat, sunglasses and a casual dress for whenever she had to go into a city where she might be recognised. With everything she needed ready to go, Eloise left behind the city where she'd lived for the past year and started out into a dangerous world where she was being hunted and had little chance of surviving, yet only one thing was on her mind and that was how the hell she was supposed to find a secret organisation that virtually nobody knew existed.

The idea struck her two months after leaving the children's home. She previously hadn't ran into any trouble and had kept mainly to fields and forests trying to figure out where 'LEP's headquarters were while also staying out of trouble and making her way around the country. But on the odd occasion that she had to enter a town she was extremely cautious and did what she had to quickly so she could leave without drawing any attention to herself. Yet one day after entering a little village right beside a forest she got attacked. A hooded man came out of an alleyway as Eloise was passing by, took a knife out of nowhere and stabbed her in the stomach. It didn't hurt her that much and it took her several minutes to realise what had happened, but it was then that Eloise knew she couldn't survive the way she was living. She was being hunted and yet had no training to defend herself. Yes she was very strong and quick at healing and the stab wound that would have hospitalised most people only felt like a bad stomach ache, but without proper training her strength was going to waste. She knew straight away that the man was part of 'LEP' as no one would just stab her and leave when she's carrying so much money. She also knew that they were probably testing her strength to see how much she could take. She thought about this on her way back to the forest and it struck her. The letter she'd found addressed to her real name was from a fighting school like her mother said and she'd been accepted. She reread the letter, sitting under an oak tree wearing her old t-shirt as she had to wash the blood out of her tank top and hoodie. It said she began first thing in September and it was August now. That left her a month to figure out how to find 'Hallow Oaks Academy'.

Eloise had no idea where to start looking for information on 'Hallow Oaks.' She checked online using a computer from a little library in a quaint town beside the beach but found nothing and was just as unsuccessful with the books. It was a week later when she started to think that she'd never find the school that she found her first lead. Eloise was going through her parents' things again to make sure they hadn't written an address somewhere when she noticed some stitching on the inside of her father's hat. It read; 'Kain-Chiko-23:47'. She knew this was left for her by her father, but was lost to what it meant. The only thing she could figure out was that '23:47' must be the time. She spent hours researching on the computer and eventually found out about a little quirky town on an island off the coast called Kain. The next day she went in search of a boat to bring her out to the island. Dressed in her dress with her make-up done and her sunhat on she went to the nearest dock to look for help. She had to be extra careful as there'd been notices in the newspaper stating her disappearance and someone could recognise her. The man at the dock was named Earendil and he said he could rent her the boat for a reasonable price but he wouldn't be able to guide her to the island. After asking if there was anyone else who could help her to get there, a younger guy maybe fifteen or sixteen with sand-coloured hair, sea-blue eyes and a sun-kissed tan, came out from the boat repair shack beside them. He looked similar to Earendil and later found out he was his son. His name was Kai. He offered to help Eloise to the island, but warned her that it could be a two-day trip.

While Kai and his father got the boat ready to set sail, Eloise sat down on the dock and looked out to sea. It would be her birthday in a day and she'd be spending it on a boat in the middle of the sea with a total stranger, a good-looking stranger, but a stranger none the less. She felt loneliness and self-pity creeping in but pushed them aside. She also felt anger at her parents, which surprised her although she understood it. They'd kept such a big secret from her, her whole life and now she had to deal with it alone. They set sail at the break of dawn the next morning. There was a slight breeze in the air as they set off into the open ocean. At first there was an awkward silence between the two of them but they slowly began talking and soon Eloise felt like she'd known Kai her whole life.

She told him things she never told anyone and he did the same. She talked about how lonely she was and he said he felt the same way as there weren't many people their age around his seaside town but how he could never leave his father and move somewhere new. Eloise could have told herself that she didn't have feelings for Kai yet she would have been lying, yet she knew they couldn't be together especially with so many secrets between them. Then out of nowhere he started telling her how his mother died. She'd been a victim of the 'Superhuman Project.' He hadn't expected Eloise to know anything about the project but when she turned around and spilled out her whole story he was shocked and sad and yet relieved that he met someone who knew exactly what he went through. He was amazed that she'd survived the experiments and could do things other humans couldn't and shocked at how she was being hunted. Eloise hadn't meant to tell him everything but felt a great weight lifted off her chest afterwards. When they arrived at the island it was like stepping into another world. There was colour and music and parties everywhere. The boat jolted slightly as they reached the lit up harbour and Eloise fell forwards so that her face was just inches from Kai's. They stayed there a moment and then she pulled away looking embarrassed although he just smiled at her, a genuine, adorable smile.

It was late when they got out of the boat. Eloise started asking around about 'Chiko', but didn't really know what she was looking for. It was at a bonfire on the beach that a man dressed in all black, looking so out of place, came up to her and whispered 'Dunne Alley', in her ear. Taking it as a clue she found Kai and asked him to help her find Dunne Alley. They found the little alleyway off a main street full of nightclubs and restaurants. It was 23:45, two minutes until she'd find whatever she was looking for. Eloise held firmly onto her dagger, which she was keeping in a hilt under her dress, but now had it in her hands. She told Kai to stay where he was and to wait for her return. The alley was dark but she could see clearly, a perk to being inhuman. It turned 23:47 and Eloise could see an old hunchbacked woman standing against a wall. This was Chiko. She didn't speak, she just simply handed Eloise a piece of rolled up paper and two plane tickets. Then she was gone. Heart pounding Eloise ran back up the street not stopping until she bumped into Kai almost knocking him over.

They went to an empty looking restaurant and got a table for two where they spent the next hour poring over the paper that Chiko had given Eloise. It was a map detailing the location of 'Hallow Oaks Academy' and two plane tickets to the country where it was situated. The two tickets puzzled Eloise. She had been the only one to meet Chiko and Kai never mentioned going to 'Hallow Oaks'.

'I'm going with you,' he said to Eloise after a brief silence. He'd gotten his acceptance letter two months before, but had never thought of leaving his father. However after meeting Eloise he felt he should go with her. His dad had other family and friends to support him and would be more than happy to see his son go to such an exclusive school.

Their plane left a week later and in that week leading up to it they had plenty of time to talk and hang out. Eloise felt herself falling for Kai, not like a teenager might think they're in love with someone and then break up with them the next week, but proper feelings. The evening before their flight they were sitting on his father's dock watching the sunset when he kissed her. She felt life and energy pouring through her like she hadn't felt before. It was like he was giving her new life and spirit and she wanted to do the same for him. She felt proper happiness for the first time in a long time and it filled her, leaving no room for guilt or grief.

The morning of their departure she watched Kai kiss his father's cheek as he said goodbye. Tears filled both his and his father's eyes, as they were overwhelmed with sadness and love. He would see him in a year, but to them it would seem like a lifetime. The plane journey was slow and quiet. Eloise knew Kai didn't want to leave his father and was probably feeling guilty about doing so, so she gave him his space. They hadn't needed their passports in the airport, which was strange, but a relief to Eloise as she didn't have a fake passport and knew they were still looking for her. Once they landed Kai became much more cheerful and they headed off towards the city centre where they caught a bus to the countryside. The bus dropped them off at an old looking bus stop in the middle of nowhere and they walked the next two miles up the road turning in at a rusted old gate, which they climbed over into an overgrown field. After walking through that field and into the next they came across what they were looking for.

An abandoned shabby building was standing alone in the centre of waist high grass and just as high weeds. The only thing that seemed to hold the building together was the ivy growing along it. The doors and windows were boarded up, but there was one loose board on a window at the back. They climbed through into a derelict hallway with three doors leading off of it. The door to the left was slightly ajar and they entered to find a wooden desk in the centre with an old man behind it. Eloise walked up to him first and showed him her acceptance letter with Kai following her to do the same. The man looked at them and then consulted a large ancient-looking book to check if they were genuine. After a couple of flicks through the book he looked up at them and smiled. 'Weren't sure if either of ye would make it,' he said to them in a croaky voice and then led them to a doorway which contained a room with just a staircase going down. 'Welcome to Hallow Oaks Academy,' he croaked in an amused sort of tone, and then he left them and went back to his desk.

The stairs led to an underground tunnel that stretched out farther than they could see. They walked in silence in the dim, damp tunnel that seemed to go on forever. They came to another set of stairs at the end of the tunnel. They ascended the stairs quickly and quietly and came out into the most amazing building ever. The roof was made of clear glass and the walls seemed to have sunlight bouncing off of them. There were people everywhere in training uniforms of varying colours showing their rank in the school. A sign saying 'New students this way' pointed to the right and Eloise grabbed Kai's arm and they followed the signs until they found themselves outside a room with both their names on it. Inside, the room was more like a lavish penthouse than a school dorm, with two separate en suites and a balcony overlooking a large courtyard filled with people sparring. Inside were two journals enclosing their timetables, a school brochure and a leaflet detailing their course. It was a 'One-Year Masters' Course for Gifted Students', according to the brochure and they seemed to be part of a very select group of students participating.

Training started first thing next day with the motto 'You won't always get breakfast before you fight.' They started straight into sparring which made Eloise nervous until she realised she could beat every participant even without skill. She fought everyone, winning each match then learning techniques she could have used instead of just force. She was top of her classes and was quickly picking up on new skills even while just watching the seniors fight outside at lunch. In the evenings she would take extra classes to learn to sneak up on people, to sense being sneaked up on and to raise her ability at stunt skills such as jumping off small heights and learn to develop her inhuman abilities. Then she'd go back to her dorm and train with Kai.

The rest of her year at Hallow Oaks was spent pretty much the same with her becoming increasingly stronger and better at fighting. Kai was doing well too and was looking forward to graduation so he could see his father again. Eloise and Kai's relationship was becoming more serious as they quickly matured through though training. At the day of graduation it broke Eloise's heart to tell Kai she couldn't go back with him, not until she destroyed 'The Superhuman Project,' and those involved. He said he understood but she could see the sadness and disappointment in his eyes. She didn't see him after graduation. By the time she got back to the dorm he had already left. She stopped herself from crying and changed her tears into anger at 'LEP' for everything it took from her. After quickly changing into her new black fighting uniform, highest in the ranks, which held a sword at her back and her dagger by her side, she packed her stuff and left, thanking those who helped her become strong. Then she made a phone call on the disposable phone she bought the year before, 'If you want me I'll be waiting,' and threw it away.

Eloise sat alone in the middle of an empty island surrounded by only grass and wind. They took longer than she'd expected but when they arrived she was ready. They came at her fast but not fast enough. She easily dogged each attack and struck back faster and harder than humanly possible. In minutes she'd taken down their whole team. But she knew better than to believe that this was all they had. Then the boss came. The man who created 'The Superhuman Project,' killed her parents and wanted to kill her. She'd become too strong for them to experiment on or research and he knew it. He congratulated her on wiping out his entire stealth team stating that they were just a trial, which made her feel sick. She wondered how such a man could live with himself after killing so many people and not even feel regret.

'But here's something you'll really love,' he smirked as he said it making Eloise's blood run cold. 'A little present for you brought all the way from Hallow Oaks Academy,' and he stepped aside to show Kai lying on the ground unconscious. This time it was Eloise's time to smirk.

'I have a little present for you too,' she said and within seconds she was beside him with her dagger up to his throat. Kai started waking up behind them, but only Eloise noticed. 'You didn't think I wouldn't know you were watching? Waiting for the right opportunity? Well you severely underestimated me and that's going to cost you,' she smiled at him as she spoke. She took in every detail of this man, the sweat around his collar, the tremble in his breath. This man was nothing more than a coward hiding behind his position, manipulating people, using cruelty to seem strong. Eloise felt no mercy for him. 'You see, Kai and I made a plan and it worked pretty well. He'd leave straight after graduation so that it would seem like we had fought and then you'd target him when he was alone to use him as leverage, but I'd know that you had him, so it wouldn't shock me into making irrational decisions like letting you go. Also, you wouldn't hurt him because if he did you knew I'd kill you, which I'm going to anyways. It's funny, if you had monitored us properly you'd have known Kai would have fought back or killed you if attacked out of the blue but I asked him to leave it to me,' She finished her explanation leaving a moment of silence for dramatic effect. Then she made the move to kill him.

'Wait!' he cried out 'I'm your father!'

'Well aren't you just full of surprises,' replied Eloise, but he cried out again, 'No really, I am your father, I dated your mother before she married someone else!'

'Well, I would ask my mother,' spat Eloise, 'but you killed her! And that "someone else" is my father, who you also killed! The man who raised me, who taught me to ride a bike, who left me a code in an old hat that helped me find the school that would train me to be able to kill you, that is my father!' Then she killed him. Without letting any more venom come out of his vile mouth she killed him and left him on an abandoned island in the middle of the sea.

That August on the day of her birthday Kai brought her out on a boat to remember their first day together. Her memories with him are the ones that help her carry on with all that she's done.

23

He's told her before that he doesn't care what she's done in the past or that she's inhuman or technically 'missing' from a children's home on the other side of the country. He told her all he cared about is their future together and that the best day to start the future is today on her birthday. Then he kissed her.

Champion is Written in my Eyes

by Finlay Wrafter, aged 14

You love to torture me with no holds barred.

It happens all the time and I find it hard.

Lose every drop of sweat,

Lose every drop of blood.

They say sticks and stones will break your bones,

Is that the reason I adore playing alone?

Yes, it is physical,

With a 'HIT' via my mobile phone.

I've had enough of all your stuff,

Same vice-versa from all relatives.

I'M LOVED!

And in my heart I am a warrior who is tough.

You are the predator and I am your prey,

Call me a lot, call me gay.

Even if I was, I would still be ok!

This little kid you're pushing around, he is trying to get away.

I was about to stand, you got me back down.

I was about to smile, you brought back the frown.

BUT NOW, it is time to grow, it is time to rise,

THE WORD CHAMPION IS WRITTEN IN MY EYES.

They can punch you and kick you,

Insult you and hurt you,

They can close every door to you,

But NEVER let people like them STOP you!

Captured in the Cornfield

by Hannah Rudden, aged 14

The man buries my feet deep into the moist soil, 'That'll do,' he noisily grunts and trudges slowly away, eventually only a speck in the distance. I take in my surroundings warily, there's corn everywhere! I've always loved corn, the smell, the taste, even the look of it makes my mouth water. The temptation is killing me. I'll have to spend the rest of my days here, a prisoner. A year passes in the torrential rain and gale force winds, my tattered hat blew off and now my hair's falling out, I fear old age is creeping up on me. Icicle-like tears sting my sagging cheeks in the winter months as I suffer from homesickness. My oversized jacket and worn trousers have torn slightly over time and have become ragged. I've never felt so weak in my life, I'm ravenous! If my feet weren't planted firmly in the ground, I would be lying on my back amongst the delicious cobs of corn, try sleeping while standing up and believe me, I need more beauty sleep than you could imagine! The only positive thing about my life is that I'm not completely alone, now and again small little birds land on my shoulders or almost bare head and fill me in on the goings on of normal life. They share stories with me about all of the things I'm missing out on such as world events, crimes, inventions, celebrity gossip and what's happening on the farm. Sometimes they carry me 'The Irish Times' or the 'Sunday Independent'. They also carry messages to and from my brothers and sisters nationwide. The birds are meant to be my enemies but everybody needs a friend. The wind is getting especially bad now, worse than it's ever been. Slowly, I feel myself being uplifted from the hardened mud, the wind taking me upwards. I hurriedly grab some corn to take with me. The man rushes into the field, starting to run after me but he's too late. This grotesque, cruel man – my captor – does not own me anymore, in fact he never did. My life will begin now. That man can scare those birds himself, I never scared them and never will. Under all this straw, I have a brain and a heart and I intend to use them, something that my captor never did.

The Quarantine Zone

by Liam Clarke, aged 15

Jack awoke suddenly. The first light of dawn spilled softly through the gaps in the grimy curtains, streaming across his chiselled features. He sat up, face in his hands, attempting to wipe the last remaining remnants of sleep from his puffy eyes. Swinging his legs over the side of the groaning pile of filthy mattresses he used as a bed, he stood up. Jack was sixteen, tall for his age. He was well-built, with bright blue eyes and matted dark hair he would often run his hand through. He bent over, splashing cold water on his face and hair from a cracked plastic bucket sitting on the dusty oak floorboards. He walked through a rotting empty doorframe into a small room that had once been a kitchen. A small wooden table was standing in the centre. A blackened kitchen worktop with wooden presses lined one wall, while the other three were bare. The wallpaper was peeling off, the plaster crumbling, revealing the brickwork underneath. Lewd drawings and swear words were scrawled on the walls. Tufts of stiff dark grass and stubborn weeds were poking up through the stained linoleum. Lying in a heap on the wooden table was a belt. A large hunting knife in a sheath and a pouch containing worn working gloves were roughly sewn to it. Jack took it and wearily fed it through the belt loops in his threadbare blue jeans. He also wore a faded check shirt, the sleeves of which were constantly rolled up above his elbows. He made his way over to the dirty wooden presses and squatted, balancing on the toes of his tattered boots. Opening the one cupboard that wasn't hanging off its hinges (the one under the sink) he lifted up the damp wooden bottom of the press, ignoring the rat droppings littering the inside of the cupboard. Once the damp piece of chipboard was removed, a small hole was revealed that had clearly been dug out from the weakened concrete. In it sat an old frayed leather bag. The leather was faded and worn. Masking tape held parts of it together. It contained Jack's most valuable possessions – things that were rare and sought after in the world he lived in. It contained things like matches, pens and paper, warm clothing, a torch, and batteries. Underneath the bag was Jack's prized possession – his beloved fibreglass recurve bow. A quiver full of arrows was strapped to the side of the leather bag. Jack came home every day and cleaned the bow obsessively with an oily rag. Now, he inserted his hand into a front pocket of the bag and retracted it, holding something small and shiny. It was a bullet. He slid it into the pouch in his belt, and began to replace the chipboard just as he heard a small scratching noise behind him. Gripping the handle of his knife, he turned slowly to see a shiny black rat scurrying across the dirty floor. It stopped at the far wall and began to gnaw at the crumbling plaster. Slowly, Jack reached back into the press and retrieved his bow. Notching an arrow quickly, he raised the bow and aimed it. It flexed appreciatively as he pulled the bowstring back and quickly released it. The arrow pierced the rat's eye socket and buried itself with a dull thud in the damp plaster. Lowering the bow, the shadow of a smile flickered across Jack's face. The plump rat ought to be worth a bullet or two. Jack retrieved the arrow, wiped it and placed it carefully back under the sink with his bow. He picked up the limp rat and slid it into the large pouch sewn to his belt. He closed the press and stood up. Heaving a long sigh, he turned around and left the one place in the world he could call home, locking the door behind him.

He now stood in a long, gloomy hallway. A cracked and dirty window that allowed shafts of greenish light to penetrate it was at the end. Ivy had claimed the building, and its searching fingers had found their way into the dank and dark rooms, through broken windows and weak brickwork. The entire building was slowly crumbling as nature reclaimed what had always been hers. Tree roots assaulted the foundations and moss and weeds were sprouting from the walls. Rotten doors hung from their hinges and the various rooms that had long ago been ransacked in search of supplies were littered with broken furniture that hadn't yet been hacked apart for use as firewood. Broken glass crunched under Jack's boots as he made his way down a dilapidated stairwell. The damp wood groaned under his weight. The morning sun, veiled behind banks of wispy cloud, was slowly ascending, taking its place in the sky. Jack shielded his eyes as they readjusted to the sudden brightness from the gloom of inside the building. The street he'd just stepped out on materialised slowly in front of him. Blinking stupidly, he surveyed the scene. The corroded remains of vehicles littered the street. The faded, broken concrete that had once been a road was disintegrating, making way for all sorts of greenery. There was a soft rustle as the gentle wind whistled through the leaves of gnarled and twisted trees, ones that had emerged from underneath concrete years ago. Jack made his way down the cracked, uneven pavement, stepping over the rubble of a house that had collapsed long ago. There was an eerie beauty about the world. It was surprisingly peaceful, witnessing nature slowly and methodically erasing every trace of a forgotten society that Jack had never known from the face of the earth. Seeing the obtrusive, grey-hued man-made world intertwined with the colourful greenery and vibrant shades of a natural living one was a sight to behold.

Turning a street corner guarded by a rusting sign, he spotted an old woman hunched over a massive steel cauldron. Her grey hair and grizzled appearance, together with her ability to make stew out of almost anything in her huge pot, had earned her the nickname, 'The Witch.' However, this old woman had a special place in Jack's heart. She was one of the few people in the entire quarantine zone that Jack could trust.

Making his way over to her, he extracted the dead rat from his pocket and laid it down on the surprisingly clean wooden worktop stacked high with plastic bowls. She didn't look up from vigorously scrubbing the inside of the cauldron. Jack cleared his throat audibly and she jumped, dropping the sodden rag into the depths of the pot.

'Jack, my boy!' she exclaimed, grinning. The mass of wrinkles on her face contorted as she revealed her stained teeth. 'What brings you to me so early in the morning?' Jack gestured to the rat lying on the worktop. She smiled fondly and picked it up. 'Right through the eye again,' she proclaimed. 'You're getting good with that bow of yours.'

Jack smiled. 'I reckon it's worth a bullet or two?' he enquired hopefully. She glanced at him dubiously before retreating into the back of her shop. Jack glanced around as he waited for her to return. The Square was slowly coming alive. The various stalls selling commodities like food, medicine, tools and materials were setting up for the day. The Square was located at the centre of the quarantine zone, or QZ as everyone who lived there called it, and was the central hub of all activity. All buying and selling was done there, and it was the place to go for the latest snippets of information and gossip. With no television, radio, or internet – things that seemed like tales from a world long forgotten to Jack – news spread like wildfire in the QZ. Gossip was all that people had for entertainment. Jack turned as the old woman emerged from her shop. She placed a small brass bullet down on the counter. Seeing the look of disappointment on Jack's face, she laughed and said, 'And a free bowl of rat stew when you come back from Labour this evening.' Jack grinned and took the bullet. Sliding it into his pocket, he turned and left, making his way over to the Kitchens.

The Kitchens were an area in the QZ where bread was handed out in the mornings and various vegetables, grown on the opposite side of the QZ, handed out in the evenings. Nearly everyone went there every morning to get a small loaf of gritty bread that was the universal breakfast in the QZ, in exchange for one bullet. Jack had woken early, and there was only a small queue when he arrived. As he dropped his bullet into the palm of the man's hand that was distributing the tough bread, the man nodded in acknowledgement. He saw almost everyone in the QZ every day, but rarely spoke. He wasn't supposed to.

Jack took his bread and ate it with some difficulty as he made his way over to the crop fields. The crop fields were located in an old park. The pavements and park benches had slowly crumbled and rotted away, leaving an expanse of open grassland. Years ago, someone had planted crops there, and now the large fields of potatoes, carrots, lettuce and wheat had to be maintained. Jack worked there every day, toiling away amid the knee- high wheat, doing his best to eradicate any weeds that dared to grow in his patch. Everyone in the quarantine zone usually participated in some form of work. This was called Labour. Those that didn't take part in Labour ran their own businesses, such as the Witch, and the people with stalls in the Square. It could be anything – working in the fields, in the infirmary, or in the Kitchens, baking bread. People were paid bullets in exchange for Labour. The crop fields were located next to the Boundary Walls, at the edge of the QZ.

Every day, Jack was watched closely by armed guards patrolling the walls, looking out over the razor wire at the city that only they ever saw. Jack's life was confined to within these walls. He had never ventured beyond them in his life, and had no desire to do so. The army that had controlled the QZ for the last twenty years constantly warned the residents by way of loudspeakers placed around the QZ of the dangers outside the Boundary Walls. The city was apparently still contaminated by the virus that had wiped out most of humanity more than two decades ago, and groups of dangerous 'bandits' roamed the city streets, scouring the dilapidated buildings for supplies and other survivors. No one in the QZ had ever seen any evidence of this, and wild theories and speculation were constantly circulating. The faceless soldiers who carried automatic weapons were never seen without their gas masks. They claimed it was to prevent exposure to the disease, but Jack was sure it was to maintain complete anonymity and to discourage anyone from talking to them. Anyway, the disease hadn't made an appearance in years. They slept in a separate area of the QZ, away from the civilians and in tents. Civilians were forbidden to go there – and you would almost certainly be shot if you did. No one knew anything about their orders, or who issued them. No one knew if they had contact with the outside world or not, or if there was any 'outside world' left. It was futile trying to talk to them. They would just constantly reassure you that everything was under control and to 'go about your business as normal.' As a result of this, people had just stopped trying to communicate with them and ignored them altogether. They were constantly there, watching and enforcing, but never fraternising with anyone that didn't have a black gas mask and body armour.

Jack looked up at one now, straightening up as he wiped sweat from his brow. The early evening sun was beating down, scorching the dry earth Jack was scouring for weeds. The man, patrolling the concrete wall, cradled his assault rifle as he surveyed whatever was beyond the wall. Suddenly, he turned, facing the crop fields, and seemed to look at Jack, who stared back. It was impossible to tell what he was looking at as his eyes were concealed behind the gas mask. Suddenly, Jack felt the man's eyes piercing him. Jack stood, unmoving, and the man's head tilted to the side, as if he was trying to understand something. Then, as quickly as it had happened, the man turned away, and resumed patrolling. Jack sighed and yanked another resilient weed from the sandy dirt.

That night, after he had finished Labour, he sat on top of the rusted hulk of what was once an upturned bus, slurping up the last of the Witches' rat stew. It had been delicious. Several people from the QZ had already personally thanked him for providing the main ingredient in tonight's stew. He had tried to hide it, but secretly he was pleased with himself. He sat there, full and content, staring at the full moon and the stars scattered across the dark sky and listening to the hubbub of chatter emanating from the Square. It was peaceful, just how Jack liked it. Suddenly, and without warning, something grabbed Jack's ankles and pulled him down from the bus. He swore colourfully, and then grunted in pain as he hit the broken tarmac face first. Instinctively, he whipped his hunting knife from its sheath and rolled over, but his attacker was already on top of him, pinning Jack's forearms to the ground with his knees. Jack struggled furiously, but it was futile.

'Hey, hey, Jack, calm down now,' laughed his attacker. 'We wouldn't want you to hurt me.' Jack stopped struggling the second he heard the voice. He opened his eyes to see the face of his best friend, Bill, inches from his own. He was grinning madly.

'You idiot!' Jack exclaimed. 'Why the hell would you do that?!'

'I was bored,' replied Bill.

'Are you insane?!' Jack shouted, still fuming. 'I could have stabbed you!' With that, Jack grabbed his empty stew bowl and

33

whipped it at Bill's head. It bounced off and reduced Bill to tears of laughter.

Half an hour later, Bill was still snickering. The two of them sat on top of the bus, making small talk. Suddenly, there was an awkward silence. Bill noticed that Jack was staring at one of the soldiers manning the wall, far away, across the Square and across the crop fields.

'You ever wonder what's out there?' Bill enquired, looking at Jack.

Jack sighed. 'Nope.'

'I do,' Bill replied. 'I hate being in here.'

'What are you talking about?' said Jack incredulously. 'It's safe in here!'

It was Bill's turn to sigh. 'You sound like that soldier on the speakers. There has not been an outbreak in over four years. Stay vigilant. Report any case of flu to your nearest official. Only YOU can keep us safe,' he mimicked in a singsong voice.

Jack sniggered, but Bill's face was set. 'You act like everything they tell us is true. I don't trust them.'

'They're just trying to keep us safe,' Jack argued.

'They're hiding stuff from us,' said Bill. 'They won't even let us see outside. It's been twenty years, Jack, since it happened. Everything could be returning to normal, to how it was before.'
'Neither of us was alive—'

'I know, Jack, but anything could be out there. If it's like what they tell us it's like, why don't they let us see? They don't want people to leave. That's why. They want people to stay here, to keep growing food and keep their little system going. They don't do any work, do they? We grow the food, prepare it... they just stand on the wall. Maybe there's no threat. Maybe they're just putting on a show of protecting us. Really they're doing nothing. Maybe humanity is rebuilding itself. Maybe the Great Flu is gone... forever.'

Jack nodded. 'That's a lot of maybe's.'

'I know,' Bill said miserably. 'I just want to know... I want to know what's out there,' he finished, staring at the moon.

'Probably just death,' said Jack. 'Just death.'

Bill left after another hour, muttering something about his mother wanting him back home early. Jack found himself sitting alone under the stars. The sound of conversations coming from the Square died down as people retired to bed for the night. Jack found himself thinking about what Bill had said, then dismissed it. Bill wasn't the sort of person to be taken seriously. Suddenly Jack sensed movement in his peripheral vision. He turned his head to see a tall, slender blonde girl walking down the cracked pavement. Jack recognised her instantly. She hadn't seen him yet. Her name was Anya, and Jack had had a crush on her since the day he first laid eyes on her. He remembered it well. Back in the early days, back when there were survivors turning up at the QZ's gates, Anya and her family had turned up on the other side of the Boundary Walls. They had entered through the huge steel gates, hands behind their heads, with at least twenty automatic weapons trained on them. Anya had been only seven and had been crying, her mother whispering soft words to her. Jack remembered wincing as Anya and her family had been roughly kicked to the ground and checked for the Great Flu using the soldiers' small device that pricked the back of the neck and checked for the flu virus by analysing the blood. Now Jack watched her, taking in her flowing blonde hair and cute face. She worked in the fields a few patches away from Jack, yet he had never really talked to her, save for an awkward 'hello' or two. Jack sighed audibly, then jumped down from the bus and returned home, where he went to bed.

The next morning, Jack slept in. He awoke with a start, instantly realising he had overslept. Hurrying into the dark kitchen, he grabbed his belt and left the room. He locked the door behind him and fastened the old leather belt as he thundered down the stairs. Suddenly, his foot caught on something that definitely hadn't been on the stairs last night. He tripped and tumbled painfully down the remaining six or seven steps, smacking his head on the exposed brickwork on the way down. He groaned in pain and then swore viciously.

'Jack....' He froze. The thing he'd tripped over was a person, propped against the wall and barely conscious. 'Jack...' the person wheezed almost silently. Jack got up and turned around. When he saw who it was, he nearly fell back down the stairs. Sadie, or as everyone knew her 'The Witch' was slouched on the stairs, pale as a ghost. Just as Jack knelt down beside her, she began to cough horribly. Her entire body convulsed as each pain-wracked cough shuddered through her. She was sweating profusely and her red-rimmed eyes told Jack she was suffering. The Great Flu was back. And it was killing her. 'You need to get out,' she told him, with great difficulty.

'Sadie...' Jack's eyes were filling with tears. This woman had taken care of him since he was a boy, had fed and clothed him. She had taken him in as her own son, after the Great Flu had killed her real one, and Jack's parents had died.

'Jack, please listen...they're going to kill everyone. They've called everyone to the Square and they're going to shoot everybody. The Great Flu, it's back... they think everyone's been exposed. It's just the South Quarter, just the South. They're going to kill everyone to stop it spreading, Jack. Take your bow and go, go... the old hotel. There's... there's an underground passage. I used to work there. The entrance is in the kitchen. The tunnel goes from the kitchen to the restaurant... it was for the waitresses. Jack... the restaurant is on the other side of the Boundary Wall. Go, now, before it's too late.' Tears were openly dripping from Jack's chin. His face was screwed up in anguish. Everything he'd ever known, his entire world, was crashing down around his ears. 'Jack... be strong. Don't die on me.'

Jack sobbed as Sadie drew her last breath. She slumped and sat there, motionless. Jack stood up, racked with sobs, and thundered up the staircase. He ran straight into his own door, splintering it and snapping it from its hinges. Ripping the door off the cupboard under the sink, he grabbed his bow and attached it to his leather bag. He slid the bag onto his shoulders and left the one place he'd called home for the last sixteen years for the very last time. Doing his very best to ignore the body on the stairs, he exploded out onto the street and began to sprint as fast as he could for the old hotel, leaping over tree roots and rusted hulks of cars. He rounded a corner and ran straight into a figure making their way to the Square, just as the first volleys of machinegun fire and screams filled the air. The massacre had begun. The person he had collided with was Anya, and as she got up he grabbed her by the arm and began to pull her along desperately.

'My parents are back there!' she screamed with terror in her beautiful eyes.

'Please, Anya... we need to go. If you want to live, follow me,' Jack pleaded. Anya sobbed desperately and nodded, and they sprinted, hand in hand, away from the gunshots, wracked with loss.

Jack kicked the rotted front door of the hotel down and they ran in, ignoring the stale musty smell. They ran down a hallway that had once been carpeted with a rich red pile, that was now faded and threadbare. The hallway was partly collapsed and they clambered over mossy plaster and brushed hanging vines aside. The gunshots echoed still through the forgotten building as they burst through the swinging doors of the kitchen. Rats scampered away as they kicked broken saucepans aside, searching for an escape. They came at last to a heavy door that was slightly ajar with a small circular window coated in dust. Grunting with effort, Jack pushed the door open and the two went inside.

A shallow stairwell was revealed. They descended, tears shining on their cheeks, and came to the bottom. Jack slid the bag off his shoulders, rummaged around in it for a second and produced a hand-powered torch. He flicked it on and it penetrated the darkness for maybe fifty feet, revealing a long, utterly black passageway. Beyond the reach of the torch beam was utter, all-consuming darkness. It was terrifying. Anya stood, trembling.

'Jack, I can't...'

Jack turned to her with a peculiar expression on his face. He took her face in his hands and looked her in the eyes. Leaning forward, he kissed her fully on the lips. They broke apart and Anya stared at him. 'Yes, you can,' said Jack simply. He turned, facing the long, empty passageway, and raised the torch. Together they walked forwards, into the darkness – in the hope of finding the light.

The Black Devil

by Darragh Murphy, aged 13

<u>Russia, Arkadak, 1549, 19th May:</u>

The scream echoed down the hospital corridor. The woman was going through a hard, painful birth. Doctors and nurses were running out of the room, all wearing the same troubled look. Another scream ripped down the corridor, sending a chill down everyone's bones. Surely a normal birth couldn't cause a woman this much pain. Olga silently sent a prayer to Saxo Grammaticus. She prayed for her daughter to have a safe birth. No one knew the father, and her daughter had only hazy memories. People were saying that she had conceived with a demon. She prayed otherwise. A new scream echoed throughout the hospital, that of a young nurse who promptly came running out with a horrified expression on her face. 'No. Dear Saxo no.' said Olga, under her breath. The doctor came out with a grim expression on his face. Olga said another silent prayer as he approached. 'I'm sorry Olga, but your daughter didn't make it.' After that, all Olga remembered was crying and blackness.

After Olga had regained consciousness, the doctor had to unfortunately give the next blow to her already frail mental health. Once she had stopped crying the doctor began to explain what had happened, 'As I have already said, your daughter died during the birth, but unfortunately she did not die giving birth to a normal child,' Olga's already heartbroken expression turned even more grave, 'What do you mean?' she asked icily. 'I mean the rumours are true ... your daughter had conceived with a demon.' The words fell like anvils from the doctor's mouth. 'The decision is yours of course as to what becomes of the infant,' the doctor paused for a moment before continuing, 'you can either take the child as your own and hopefully you find that only it's appearance is demonic, or you can decide not to take the risk and send him into the mountains to freeze to death.' It was a long time before Olga responded, 'As you can see doctor, I am far too old to have another child, that and with my husband dead there is no chance of me having another child. But I'll be damned if I'll let my family line run dry. That child may be the last of my line so I'll accept this child as my own. If it becomes like his father then we have strong men here. I'm sure it won't be too hard to send it back to his father.' 'Of course,' the doctor replied. 'Let us go and see your new child.

Olga had to fight hard to hold her tears in check. The doctor was right, the boy was monstrous. Every part of him was black as coal, all apart from his eyes, which were blood-red. He had two tiny horns growing from his forehead. His feet ended in nails that were sharper than any of the doctor's own tools. The same could be said for his hands, which had three fingers that ended in razor sharp claws. The doctor's voice made her involuntarily flinch, 'Are you sure you wish to keep the child?' Olga nearly let loose a tear, 'No, but I'm taking it... him with me all the same.' Surprisingly the doctor started to chuckle, Olga wanted to smack him, 'Why do you laugh? Do you think me simple?' the doctor stopped chuckling but still had an amused tone, 'No, no Olga, it is just when I left my home in Kazakhstan, my friends and family said that I'd not get more excitement in another country, this has surely proved them wrong has it not my good woman?' Olga could not help but start to laugh. Soon they were both howling with foolish laughter. And in their laughter they had failed to notice the infant had sat up and now stared curiously at them.

Thirteen years later:

The boy had grown to be an immensely strong and intelligent young boy. Contrary to his appearance, the boy had the heart of an angel. Instead of using his strength to bully others, he spent his time helping the adults and protecting the other children. And sometimes adults as well, as he had proved last month, by heroically grappling the giant mountain bear that had tried to kill the wood cutter Marat. He had wrestled the bear into submission, picked up Marat's axe and drove it though the beast's head. The bear had been a fine feast and there was enough to leave the whole village full and content. Unfortunately he was still bullied and cast

40

down for his appearance, but due to his personality, he didn't raise a hand or his voice in return. Now it just so happened that a month after the boy was born, in which time he was called Olaf, a blind girl was born. She was named Lidiya. She and Olaf had been friends since infancy, due to the fact that she could not see his demonic form. Although Lidiya's mother had forbid her seeing the demon-spawn, as she so often called him back then, they had always snuck out to see each other until the mother had eventually agreed to the friendship as Olaf's true personality had shone through.

All this raced through Olaf's head as they sat on the hill, staring out at the stars. Lidiya turned to Olaf and whispered in his ear. 'I think I love you.' Olaf was too stunned to speak for a moment, 'But I'm a monster,' he exclaimed angrily, 'a beautiful girl like you could never marry a demon like me.' 'Oh Olaf,' she exclaimed 'Are you too stupid to realize I don't care for looks! I love you for your personality. Sometimes I think it is you who is truly the blind one, you old fool!' Lidiya's hand snaked through the grass towards his. Olaf couldn't help but notice how smooth and cool her hand was against his hot, stone-like hand. He turned around to protest but instead Lidiya's lips touched his. 'I love you Olaf.' 'I love you too Lidiya.' They kissed again and looked out at the stars. No other word was spoken that night. Eventually sleep welcomed them in its warm embrace.

Nine years later:

Olaf was tilling the last of the field. Lidiya was milking the last of the cows. Life was good for Olaf. He was married to Lidiya; they had a large farm with Nanny Olga living happily retired with them. And soon, according to Sitar, the doctor who had pulled him out of his mother's womb, Lidiya would soon give birth to a child. There were a few murmurs wondering if Lidiya would die during the birth like Olaf's own mother. But these were soon expelled from their minds as Olaf's mother had been extremely sick and exhausted. Life was good.

One day while Olaf was out hunting, a troop of soldiers had come through the village. The captain, an extremely cruel, bitter man, had seen Lidiya and had immediately fallen for her. He asked the leader of the village, a wise old man called Pavel, was she taken. He had said yes and the captain had flown into a rage. When the captain had cooled down a bit he said if 'I can't have her then no one can'. He knocked Pavel unconscious and rode out to the farm. He asked her to leave her husband behind. She, of course being very loyal to Olaf, had said no, at the same time Olaf had come back from the hunting trip with a large grin on his face. He had come in the door just as the captain had drawn his sword and drove it straight through Lidiya's stomach. Olaf ran into the house, picked up the captain and flung him out the door. He knelt down beside Lidiya and gingerly picked her up. Tears streamed down Olaf's face as he regarded his dying wife. 'Olaf,' she said weakly, coughing on her own blood, 'Yes Lidiya?' he whispered as though speaking too loud would kill her faster. Lidiya sucked in her last breath and whispered, 'I love you.' She released her pent up breath and travelled into oblivion. 'I love you too.' He whispered. Suddenly his sorrow turned to red-hot anger. He stood up and marched outside. The captain, both legs broken, was trying to crawl away. Olaf picked him up by the neck and pushed his face into the captain's face, 'You killed my wife and my un-born child.' The captain whispered, struggling to push each word out. 'Please show mercy.' Olaf responded coldly. 'Sorry, my mercy died with my love.' With seemingly no effort, Olaf tore the man limb from limb and then left him to bleed to death. Consumed by grief and rage, he turned on the rest of the village. He killed everyone, every child, every elder, every domesticated animal. Even his old grandmother, Olga. When he was done he burned the village down. Standing in the midst of the ruins that were once his home, he began to cry, each tear landing on his huge chest and dripping to the snow below. Suddenly, a black silhouette appeared in the smoke. A deep voice rang out, dripping with pure evil, 'I was beginning to doubt you were of my loins at all.' 'Father?' Olaf called out. The dark voice replied mockingly, 'Yes my son. I am your father and you shall bow down to me.' The voice was so compelling that Olaf dropped to his knees. 'You shall cast away the name that has been given to you. From now on you will be my knight, my thug if you will. And as such I name you

The Black Devil.' Olaf's voice sounded weak after his father's booming voice, 'Yes father.'

'Who are you?'

'The Black Devil.'

'Louder boy!'

'I AM THE BLACK DEVIL!!!'

Monopoly

by Lauren Hannon, aged 14

She sat in her kitchen, as she usually did on a Wednesday afternoon, watching her young daughters play. They had found a pair of dice and decided to make their own fun. She watched them, as she usually did. They rolled the dice, laughing and smiling. She suddenly thought back to the games she played when she was their age. They were different. So different.

The vividness of the memory, even after all those years had passed, haunted her. He rolled the dice: two twos. He moved her token and brought her to there. She was four years old. She stood outside their bedroom door, listening to their argument. They screamed at each other. She would try to hold back the tears but she never was good at being strong. She thought they heard her so she ran to her room to hide. Her blonde hair was in a million knots and her face was red. She lay down with the blankets placed over her and pretended she was a princess in a castle, waiting to be saved. She felt safe; she thought that the monsters couldn't get to her there.

The screams of laughter brought her back to reality.

'Mum, will you play the game with us?' her youngest daughter begged.

'Maybe later, girls,' she replied.

'Mum, please,' the both squealed.

'Okay, but only for a few minutes, then you've to do your homework'

She sat down on the floor and the girls began explaining how the game worked to her. They were so excited that their mother decided to play. She never usually played games with them. She said she didn't like games. They passed her the dice and she rolled them. She shut her eyes and instantly, as the dice dropped to the floor, the first feeling of control she had ever felt all those years ago when she had taken the dice off him, came back to her.

She was a little girl again. Nine years old. She had landed on Chance. She thought this was it; she thought that she could finally be who she needed to be. The small card gave her something she wished for everyday: confidence. The monsters were still around but she was happier. The Monopoly board didn't seem so sinister, now that she was winning. She felt like she finally understood how to play the game. Teachers started to like her, and she began to like school. She stopped crying in school; she cried enough at home. She felt less weird though, she felt that maybe she could have a normal life after all. Just as she took control of one monster, another one came along. He took her Chance and ripped it into shreds. She was back at the beginning.

'Mum, it's your turn again,' the girls excitedly screamed.

'Oh, what?' she said, startled by their sudden interruption to her thoughts.

'It's your turn, Mum.'

'Oh, okay.' She picked up the dice, her hands shaking.

'Are you okay?' her eldest daughter asked.

'Actually no, I think it's time we stopped playing and you both start your homework.'

'Can we just do it for five more minutes?' the younger girl begged.

She didn't have the heart to refuse.

'Fine,' she replied, her voice unsteady.

She picked the dice off the floor and got ready to roll them again. She looked at her two children who were sitting in front of her. Their hopeful faces made her think of the first hope she had of having a normal, happy life. When she thought she had control again, she was eleven years old. She slowly removed him from her life. The other monster wasn't so bad anymore. 5th class. She was always smiling. She had a lot of friends and she was happy. She loved school. Her favourite subject was Maths. She liked how the problem always had a solution. School became her escape. Her best friend told her a secret. She suddenly realised no one was perfect. Everyone had their own monsters.

She rolled the dice onto the floor for the last time in the innocent little game. She remembered the last time he had control. She was fourteen years old. She was afraid of the dark. She would see him in her constant nightmares. How did she keep losing control of his game? He said that the game was life. That couldn't be life. He could continue playing games. He could stay on the Monopoly board but she had enough, she had enough of allowing other people to roll the dice for her. He could win or lose the game but she was no longer playing, she was just living.

The thoughts of the games she played when she was younger faded from her mind. She looked at her girls, still completely engrossed in their little game. They didn't have a care in the world. She felt a smile rising somewhere inside.

'His game is over,' she whispered to herself.

The Were War

by Grace Cassidy, aged 14

My dad is the Alpha of the Shadow Howlers pack, one of the strongest packs in the world. Because he's the Alpha we lived in the huge pack house. One evening as I walked in from school my mom shouted, 'You better hurry up and get ready, pack training starts in an hour.'

'But we don't have training until tomorrow.'

'No your father has increased it to every day now because of all these Rouge attacks. The Night Moon Pack got attacked the other day. They said the Rouges are really strong, they injured the Beta!' mom told me worriedly.

'Shift now,' my dad commanded in his Alpha tone. Soon, the whole clearing was filled with wolves of all different colours, ranging from dark browns to blonds, from greys to reds. And then there was me, the only white wolf. Dad set us doing some fighting drills and walked off, leaving his Beta, Brian, in charge. I'm a good fighter, but I've a short temper so I have to be careful.

Suddenly, a bunch of wolves burst in on us, snapping and snarling. From the smell of them, they were Rouges. There were around thirty of them. Numerically, we were evenly matched. They jumped onto us, biting, tearing and snapping viciously. The clearing was filled with growls and yelps and the smell of blood. We tried the best we could to fight them off, but we were disorganised and unprepared. Like a grey shadow, dad leaped into the clearing and pulled a Rouge off me, snapping its neck and throwing it to the side. The Rouges, having spotted dad, took off running back into the forest. Dad, Brian and some of our strongest fighters went after them. I went around the clearing, checking on the other wolves. Everybody was cut and bitten, but thankfully nobody was seriously injured. I leaned against one of the trees and tried to catch my breath. The third in command, Luke, told us all to go home, or if we needed, to the pack doctor.

The next morning I got up and stretched, feeling bruises all over my body. I went downstairs and got breakfast. In the kitchen, I found mom. She caught hold of my face and her sky-blue eyes searched my green ones worriedly.

'You alright?' she asked.

'Course I am,' I replied.

'Ok. Your father has called a pack meeting. It starts in half an hour.'

I hurried to the meeting, slightly late, and found Dad ending his speech to the pack.

'And we will win this war!' he shouted. Everyone started shouting, yelling, and cheering excitedly.

'We meet in the training clearing this evening at six. I've contacted the other packs and three are willing to help, Night Moon, Shadow Fang and Windrunner!'

'We're starting a war?' I asked dad once the pack had left.

'Not really a war, just one big battle to end it all,' he said, walking out of the room.

That evening, I headed to the clearing. All the packs were there, waiting. Without any warning the Rouges attacked. It had started. There was way more wolves this time, the previous attack must have been a tester group. My mind raced. I heard the sickening crunch of bone, there was fur flying everywhere, blood splattering and wolves biting and growling. Grab a Rouge, kill it, move on. As I fought I could see my comrades and enemies fall, never to rise. I heard them whining, yelping, screaming and crying. Sounds of pain and the smell of death pervaded the clearing. Then, a big black wolf walked out, calmly observing the battle. His head snapped to the side and he saw dad finishing off another Rouge. With a ferocious snarl he charged over and snapped Dad's neck. I let out a howl before my vision went red. I sprang at the black wolf, blind in my rage, He sidestepped then jumped at me, I dodged, turning around quickly. But not fast enough, he jumped at me again, claws outstretched, and I knew I wasn't fast enough. He landed on me and everything went black.

'If I knew then what I know now...'

by Patrick Sweeney, aged 15

As I opened the rusty, old gates of the empty graveyard, death outstretched its arms to me and it grew closer with every breath I took. The deafening silence was broken as I walked through the rustling leaves at my feet below. I brought with me a single red rose. It stood out against the bleakness of the graveyard like the moon against the blackened night sky. When I finally found the gravestone with the familiar epitaph, I immediately regretted coming here at all. The memories of the soul lying underneath this slab of rock came flooding back to me, and there was nothing I could do to stop them...

It was a bright, crisp Saturday morning and the dew of the morn lay on the sweet green grass, like a soft blanket covering the harshness of the world. I awoke to the sound of little Jim demanding his breakfast from his cot next door. Mary lay beside me, still in a state of dream. She had been told to rest herself as her bones were weakening fast and the cancer was spreading at a quicker rate than expected. I left her to sleep. She always looked so perfect when she slept. As I entered the kitchen downstairs, I was met with the stench of burnt toast. It was Aoife's attempt of breakfast. Jim crunched up his face and blocked his nostrils being the drama queen that he was. I opened the window and put on a fresh batch of toast. Aoife rarely made mistakes so I let her off easy. She gave me a great huge smile. Her whole face lit up when she smiled. Nathan was glued to his new Xbox game, something that was becoming a habit of his. He slouched out of the sitting room and propped himself up for breakfast. His eyes rolled around the back of his skull. Mary came down and joined us too. She was still at the early stages of cancer yet and was very mobile. Our breakfast was an enjoyable one, the last breakfast we would have together as a family. How I sincerely wish things turned out differently.

Aoife decided she wanted to go to the Aquarium, which had just opened recently. Nathan thought it was a great idea (for a change) so I decided I would bring them. Mary said she'd give it a skip. 'I'll stay here love, Jim and I will catch up on Fireman Sam'. Jim was about to intervene, but was distracted on hearing the familiar theme song of his favourite fireman. The Aquarium was packed. Young kids ran loose from wall to wall, watching the sea creatures soar around their heads. Aoife was mesmerised. She couldn't believe the wide variety of animals that existed. Nathan tried not to let too much emotion show. He wanted to keep the 'cool kid' act going, although he was surrounded by younger, wilder kids. After two hours of wandering around the Aquarium, I decided it was time to go. Aoife reluctantly agreed and waved good-bye to all the sea creatures. Everything was great, until the journey home.

Mary was cleaning up at home. She decided she was going to surprise us for when we got home and have dinner ready for us. She rarely did the cooking for us so spaghetti Bolognese was a big feat for her, too big of a feat. Jim was in the sitting room, belting out the lyrics of Fireman Sam to the best of his ability. But that didn't stop him hearing the high-pitched scream coming from the kitchen. Mary was lying there, drenched in the boiling water from the spaghetti. Her flesh was being burnt away with every second that passed. How I wished Jim didn't have to witness such a horrific site. Gaudy burns covered his mother's fragile body as she lay in a heap. She was barely breathing and was in no state to go get help. Jim knew what he had to do. He ran for help in such a state of shock he didn't look where he was running. He was heading for next-door's house across the road, but we were heading home.

We were five minutes from home and the arguing started. Aoife and Nathan were debating about the sea creatures and the aquarium. Nathan persisted in telling her that they were all captured from their homes and taken from their families, while Aoife tried to ignore him and his malicious tone of voice. I had to intervene. Aoife was nearly in tears by the time I turned around. It was the greatest mistake of my life. It only took a split second to turn, to cease the argument, and to hit the child. When I realised I had hit something, I didn't know what it was. I nearly laughed for a minute as I thought to myself, 'That's the third cat you've hit this year!' If only it was a cat.

We got out of the car, all expecting to see some dead furry animal. Then we saw it. A small, blue shoe. The size of shoe Jim would wear. His favourite colour too. It was Aoife who reacted first. She ran to the house and into the kitchen, where she found her mother. Still lying there, still breathing thank God. But Aoife couldn't tell her mum. She couldn't bring herself to do it. It wasn't until several days after in the hospital that Mary found out her youngest son was killed by her own husband. Nathan just stared in disbelief. He said nothing but eventually left the corpse of his little brother in the arms of his dad and walked off. Jim looked like he was simply asleep. He just lay, lifeless in my arms. He wasn't cut, or marked, but just left with a small poppy bruise. That was the last memory I have of that day, the rest is a blur...

Every year I come to this lifeless graveyard and sit here with little Jim. I think about that heart rendering day and how I tore my family apart in a matter of seconds. Mary left me, and took the kids with her. She blames me for what happened to Jim, and what happened to her. I have nothing now but this single red rose. In a way, it's a symbol of my love for Jim, but also a symbol of grieving. As I leave it on the cold slab of cement, I leave with it the memories of his death. One day, this graveyard will be my home, but there will be no one to bring me a rose.

Late Impressions

by Kate Ryan, aged 14

Of the few people he expected to meet, she wasn't one of them. Annie Taylor was there in front of him, looking like something out of a perfume ad. Her face was turned, her piercing blue eyes glassy and distractedly staring into the distance. She was probably thinking of something so complex and poetic, something Damien knew he would never be able to imagine. It was cold and Damien held his arms tightly hoping the pressure would miraculously warm them up. They didn't and he was left to shiver. He looked at her again while he was still invisible and wondered how anyone could look so cool leaning up against a dirty alley wall.

Annie had one arm across her chest while the other rested on it, two fingers held to her lips, which still looked great, despite the red lipstick being a little smeared, as she encased a skinny little cigarette between them. She inhaled deeply and confidently; the black jacket zipped up her chest heaving gently as she did. The way she looked in that sleek, black dress that skirted above her knees as she smoked, reminded Damien of the Femme Fatales in the noir film posters he plastered across his bedroom walls. She looked so cool, unlike the girls at school as they huddled at the back of the school passing a cigarette between them, spluttering and coughing, as soon as it touched their lips.

'Can I bum a smoke?' Damien said as he studied the cracks on the pavement, making a bit of an effort to sound unfazed by it all.

Annie jerked, looked at him big eyed and startled, but she set into a warm smile as soon as Damien felt her eyes cease to scan him. Suddenly embarrassed, his hands fell into the comfort of his pockets and clung tightly to his sides.

'Yeah, sure,'

The cigarette was now lightly clasped in the side of her mouth as she dug downwards into the black leather bag dangling from her. The streetlamp shone on the back of her head making the blackness of her hair look a fluorescent orange. Dressed in black, she could even fade into the sombre night, if you weren't concentrating on her. But he was. When she found it, she was struck with a sigh of giddy satisfaction and stumbled cheerily over as she held out a shaky arm to hand it to him. He held it softly in his hand, so afraid he would drop it, as if it would smash into a million golden diamonds that would scatter across the slick, black tarmac.

She must have one class fake to get these. Damien had just got his from his friend James, who apparently really had the underworld connections he always joked about. It looked so professional at the time, even if the ink was a little smudged and the picture a little faded. He didn't say it to James, who spent weeks buzzing in anticipation, as he conjured up all the Jersey Shore worthy antics, he'd get up to. He squeezed Damien's shoulders and promised him a world of craic, if he came with him tonight. The bouncer raised eyebrows and likely considered turning them away, even though he thought he looked grown-up in the jacket he borrowed from Dad and the jeans he bought new for the occasion. But only so much skinny teenager you can hide in a smart jacket.

The bouncer begrudgingly waved them in, likely convinced by James' stocky, rugby player build and the fact he looked twenty despite being sixteen.

Damien had quickly decided it wasn't his scene with the pulsing generic pop that could be felt in your throat, the pink lights and the hazy smoke that followed them. But worst of all the strategic effort, you had to put in to walk five steps. He made his way out the closest fire exit and here he was.

'Hey, don't ya go to my old school?'

Damien was snapped into reality by her loud inquiry and found himself confused at the warmth in her tone. Her eyes were still wide, slightly dazed and her smile still bright, as she gazed at him, seemingly interested. So completely unlike her.

'Yeah, Damien Clarke, you're Annie Taylor, right?' he asked, attempting to be deadpan.

'Tis me,' she said as she threw her hands up dramatically, wobbling a little bit on her high heels.

'I thought it was you, I haven't thought of the place in ages, not much of a fan, little boring for my taste, not that it's any less in my new one.' The words came pouring out of her mouth with little breath between words, her voice high and fast yet still a little hoarse. It was probably the most she ever said to him. Not that she was ever mean or cold, but she was just disinterested in everything really. Spent most of her time staring out the window, yet still managing full marks in tests. She kept to herself in class, quiet and when called upon to answer she would quickly mutter the right answer while her face flushed red as if it was wrong. Her arms had a permanent spot across her chest and only left when she was laughing loudly among her small group of older friends, who she'd known since childhood and who kept to the corner table in the lunch room.

Damien never figured out why he noticed her this much, maybe it started when he sat beside her in French and leaned over to copy, only to notice the lyrics of a Nirvana song scrawled in the margins. That was his favourite band and none of his friends seemed to care about them.

Yet here was this smart, painfully shy girl blabbering and was clearly drunk or high, so unlike her. He heard a few rumours, but didn't pay much attention to them. She looked as if she barely knew what she was saying herself as she continued speaking. Now, he noticed how reliant she was on the wall to keep steady. Maybe this was a once-off thing, he certainly hoped so; it would be pretty bad if she threw herself away because of crap like that. Noticing the shaking of her legs, he realised she was about to fall. He quickly grabbed her slender body. Annie's head fell softly onto her shoulder and he could smell the sour scent of drink melding with the smoke. Her hand was placed gently on his jaw, and the feel of her fingerprints made him shiver a little, but he barely thought about it. The expression on her face was so dazed and faraway, he doubted she even knew what she was doing. The loud squeaking of the fire escape made him jump so much, he almost dropped her. She still hung almost lifelessly in his arms.

'What are ya at?' A large silhouette barked at him from the door. As he hustled closer, Damien could see the stony purse of his lips and furrowed brow, and instantly realised he was Annie's boyfriend.

'Nothing, I mean, she was about to fall.' Damien quickly protested, embarrassed at the squeaky break in his voice as he did. The hulking guy came over to him, nostrils flaring and roughly grabbed Annie. Annie looked up, smiling and wrapped her arms loosely around his neck. She still looked pretty sick and Damien wasn't sure about this guy's judgement. He didn't look like a corrupter of innocence with his smart enough dress and clean-shaven face. He didn't have messy black hair or dark brooding eyes. Still that angry glint in his eyes and the curled fists suggested he was meaner than you'd think. Summoning up the courage, he stepped closer and looked him hard in the eyes.

'Look, she's really out of it and doesn't seem to be in good form, you better take care of her.'

'Don't you try to start with me, you don't know anything.' Her boyfriend said while taking a hard shove at Damien. Damien felt the sharp tension now building in his shoulder and realised there was little he could do. She barely knew him and he barely knew her too. Maybe this boyfriend of hers was just being a little overly protective, but either way it's not like Damien would be able to phone her a cab or anything, he didn't know where she lived. So he just put his arms up defeating and let them saunter off.

When the door slammed and Damien was left in the cold, he felt the smooth shape of the cigarette carton resting in his hand. He turned it over a few times, and then opened it. He tipped it and let every cigarette fall to the ground. He could feel the paper break and the ash spilling out, breaking up softly beneath his twisting shoe. He hoped she would get home okay and began to walk back into the pulsing club, hoping to find James. He slipped the carton into his pocket as the door closed behind him.

The View From the Other Side

by Ciara Hennessy, aged 15

1

It was my first time away from my home and family. It was a new start, a new me. I should have just kept myself to myself, but all I wanted to do was help. I think I'm just too kind for my own good!

Let me introduce myself. My name is Thomas Blake-Burke-Wolfe. My friends – when I had any – used to call me Tom. I come from a very noble and well-respected background of Wolfes. We have lived in the forest for a very long time. The name 'Wolfe' used to mean a lot around these parts of the country. Not since I came along! I blame it on the Three Little Pigs and their lies! They started it! Then everyone jumped on the bandwagon. Now I'm known everywhere as 'The Big Bad Wolf'. People hiss and boo when I pass, but what happened wasn't my fault. I'm a very nice wolf really, but lately everything that happens is blamed on me. I'm the innocent victim of circumstances, and that's why I want to set the record straight.

I remember well, the first spot of bother I had with these three porkers. It happened shortly after I had moved to the forest; I was on my way to visit old Mrs Riding Hood's house, as I heard she wasn't at all well. I thought I'd take her out to lunch to cheer her up. I'm just that kind of bloke! So I arrived anyway, and I let myself in – she keeps her key under the flower pot- next thing the old biddy started to scream at the top of her voice!

'Help! Help! It's the Big Bad Wolf! "

The Big Bad Wolf? Who? Me? It was the first time any one had ever called me that! I was gobsmacked! Try as I might I could not stop her squealing like a Sioux Indian.

'Dear Lady,' I cried, 'I just want to have you for Dinner!'

Well that went down like a lead balloon!

58

'HELP! HELP! THE BIG BAD WOLF IS GOING TO EAT ME FOR DINNER!!'

It struck me a second too late! I said... 'To have you for dinner' ...I had meant to say to "bring you out for dinner". The damage was done! The old bird screamed and shrieked and wailed until my ears rang. In the end I turned desperately to flattery.

'My, my, what big eyes you have! ...What big ears you have! ... What long –'

Just then, something else hit me; a big heavy frying pan! Luckily I caught it, or it would have sliced my head off! I was half in and half out dodging boiled sweets, knitting needles and hair rollers when who should come along, only these three pigs. With one look at me, they laughed and disappeared into the forest, only to return, with the old boot's nephew, the woodcutter, and his sister; Red Riding Hood. The woodcutter was waving an axe the width of a church door, and Red Riding Hood was shouting such vile abuse I had to cover my ears with my paws. To make a long story short I escaped within an inch of my life. Of course I told everyone the truth... But do you think anyone believed me? That little vixen Red Riding Hood went around telling everyone that I had tried to gobble up her old defenceless Granny, false teeth and all. How nasty can you get!!!

From that day on, it was downhill all the way. Thomas Blake-Burke Wolfe had become the Big Bad Wolfe. The Three Little Pigs (brothers I suspect) were all over the place, telling the sheep where I was hiding and reporting me to the police if I so much as looked at a hen! Little Miss Muffet – I used to think she was such a lovely child – threw a rotten orange at me, when my back was turned. I came across her the following day sitting on a tuffet outside Mr Humpty Dumpty's house. She was eating her lunch – a steaming hot bowl of curds and whey. I tipped my hat as I passed her and exchanged small talk with Mr Dumpty who was out pruning his roses. Later I was informed that there were a certain three brothers noticed at the scene of the crime. As I walked on, I heard a blood-curdling scream. I spun around to see a much-traumatised Little Miss Muffet. She frightened me so much that I tripped and fell. In her hysterics, Little Miss Muffet spilled sticky curds all over my new tweed jacket! To make matters worse, Mr Dumpty who had climbed on to the wall to get a better view was knocked off, in a most vile and vicious fashion-a stone thrown by the oldest of those three ruffians. Before you could blink, all hell broke loose. The unfortunate egg was lying helplessly in bits and all the kings' horses and all the kings' men were dashing round trying to put him back together again. Anyone who wasn't picking up bits of egg was trying to restrain a frantic Miss Muffet, who wouldn't shut up about a spider. Then the most shocking thing happened! I was called in on suspicion for the crime, and the only person who could clear me was gone in an ambulance!

I was really at my wits end, a shadow of my poor self. I really wished I was back home with my family, but it was out of the question. I swear, I wasn't even there the day Bo-Peep lost her sheep; she was probably off frolicking with Boy Blue! Don't even get me started on Jack & Jill! I'd bet my sweet aunt it wasn't water that was in that pail! And I was at flower arranging at the time! When anything happens the police no longer say, 'round up the usual suspects', they say 'round up the usual suspect' – ME! Apparently I am 'wildly out of control'.

On the afternoon that I was released from prison on bail, I was walking down the lane when I heard a peculiar drilling noise – my first thought was that I was reacting badly to the pills the vet had given me for my nerves, but as I walked on I saw that those Three brats (for use of a better 'B' word) unloading all kinds of stuff off a lorry. They were starting a construction right opposite my house. I swear a light bulb lit up over my head! Oh by God I'd have them! I grabbed my jacket and high-tailed it down to the County Council. Closed on Sundays. Drat. Not giving up, I spent days and days patiently waiting for their stupid houses to be built. Finally the day came – D-Day.

I put on my finest attire and strolled down to the old rasher-heads. I had all my legal firms organised; colour-coded and laminated, my evidence; they were going down.

As I strutted cockily up their drive, three heads emerged from behind a curtain, sniggering in a most annoying fashion that made you want to smack them. I puffed out my chest and knocked on their door. No reply. At this point my noise was twitching from the cold, and my fur was blowing higgledy-piggledy in the rough wind. It grew stronger and I could hardly breathe, I had to huff and puff to get some air into my lungs. As for keeping balance, it was impossible. I staggered and leaned against the door for support, still huffing and puffing. Suddenly, the whole house fell in. I swear, I had nothing to do with it! It just collapsed! Well, it just shows what will happen when you let amateurs build a house with inferior materials, and without planning permission!!! Of course the three swine scurried down to the County Council, (which by the way was open – it was Tuesday). I was charged with breaking and entering and damaging private property. I got one hundred and fifty hours of community service! Gosh darn it! Worse was to come, there was a house warming party, (which I was uninvited to). Every pig in the place was there, and anyone who was anyone; The Three Blind Mice, Pinocchio, the Fairy Godmother, The Three Bears and Goldilocks, Snow White, Cinderella, Peter Pan, Tinker Bell, Bo Peep, Little Boy Blue, Miss Muffet and that awful cat and the fiddle. He didn't stop playing that screechy thing all night! I didn't get a wink of sleep. The wild party went on into the early hours of the morning, until I heard the blissful sound of car doors slamming shut and drunken shouts of 'Goodbye'. I had had enough, so I got out bed and stormed down. I banged on the door and one of the pigs, (don't ask me which one) – they all look the same to me – opened the door. He had Snow White on one arm and Cinderella on the other. He winked at me, and then slammed the door in my face. The absolute cheek of him! A half an hour later I was arrested for trespassing, and do you know what my community service was??? I had to clean up the rubbish from those horrid hogs party!

There are always two sides to every story. For me, it's always the same old story. It's not true! This is my version. Please believe me, and don't ever be too quick to judge!!

The Unholy Trinity

by Kate Moore, aged 14

'I get obsessed with girls very easily. It only ever lasts a couple of days, mind.'

'So that's me, yeah?' I grinned. He looked very earnest behind those incredibly large glasses.

'No, actually.'

'Right. Why?'

'What's your name again?'

'Trinity.'

'That's why.'

'So why are we on a date? Here, of all places.' I wrinkled my nose at the red-white-and-blue All American Diner with the middle-aged, overweight men in the corner and the short-skirted waitress. It wasn't really my kind of place. I told him so.

'If I'm paying,' he replied simply, 'Which I'm not, by the way, I can't actually afford anywhere else, so, sorry darling, but you're going to have to put up with it.'

'I don't see why.'

'I guess you're used to tête-à-tête luncheons, yeah?'

'I'm sorry. I don't speak French.' I said coldly.

'I'm surprised. My sister does, and she's a lot politer than you. I don't actually want to be here, you know.'

'So why are you?'

'I'm beginning to wonder why I should tell you.'

'You should.'

'Should I?'

'Yes! You should. Or I'll leave.'

'Go ahead.'

He waited. I stayed put.

He gave a quick smile. 'Thought so. I'm not here for you. I'm here for my mate, who is also not here for you, but is at home for you.'

'That makes no sense.'

'Only because you're narrow-minded.'

'What? I am not narrow-minded!'

'Yeah, you are.'

'Did you just come here to insult me? Because if you did, I'll just go home. I don't even know your name!'

'Darrell. Darrell Ligate.'

'Isn't Darrell a girl's name?'

'Not where I come from.' Darrell stood up. He was incredibly skinny, I realized. Like a stick. And tall, maybe six foot. I think the word I'm looking for is 'weedy'. He had messy, brown hair in a fringe, hooded brown eyes, and those glasses I mentioned. He wore a shirt, suit pants and black shoes covered in dried mud.

'Why are your shoes muddy?'

'Is that really the point of this conversation?' He pulled up his trousers.

'No, but you won't tell me what is, so.'

'You're not very patient are you?' he sat back down. 'Alright, I'll tell you.'

'Well?'

'My friend wants to go out with you.'

'What?' I couldn't help it, it was my initial reaction.

'My friend wants to go out with you.'

'It wasn't that kind of "what"!' I was kind of appalled.

'Why do you sound so horrified?'

'Because he asked you to ask me!'

He shrugged. 'So?'

Boys.

But still...

'What does your friend look like?'

'You're such a hypocrite.'

I chose to ignore this comment. I pushed my long, straight hair out of my eyes and leaned forward. 'Well?'

He gave an exasperated sigh. 'Go see for yourself. He pulled a piece of paper out of his pocket and shoved it into my hand. A mobile number was inked on it in small blue letters.

'Umm...'

'It's his number, idiot.'

'Hey!' But he was already heading out the door. 'I don't even know his name!'

'Simon!' And he was gone.

I headed for the bathrooms, pulling my phone out of my pocket. Once in a cubicle, I dialled the number.

***

Simon was angry. With himself.

'You angry, Anderson? Frustrated?'

'No.' But his fists were clenched.

'You sure?'

I should be able to deal with this, thought Simon. I should be able to deal with this!

In fairness, he thought afterwards, it's kind of difficult. My arms are pinned behind my back. That's the excuse I'll make to Darrell.

'Well, Anderson? Are you angry?'

'No!'

'You sure you're sure?'

The teenager pinning his arms behind his back in an increasingly painful position was tall, burly, and incredibly strong. He had a skinhead and a boring t-shirt. This much Simon had noticed.

'I'm sure!'

'But honestly?' It hurt. Simon struggled, but this guy's grip was iron. They were in the school bathroom too, so there was barely anyone around, and those that saw them hurried quickly past, staring at the ground. He couldn't quite place this guy.

'What's your name again?'

'You don't even know my name! You're so full of knowledge, but you don't even know my flippin' name!'

He didn't say flipping, though,

'It was pretty basic, Mr – er –'

Mr-whatever-his-name-was shook him.

'Flippin' know-it-all!'

The whole argument had started over Simon knowing about the solar system. In science, the teacher had asked them about the solar system. 'Does anyone know how big the planets are? Biggest to smallest?'

'Umm... Saturn, Jupiter, Uranus?'

'Ha! He said Uranus! Sir! Tom said Uranus!'

'Does Pluto count?' This was Simon.

'Does Pluto count?' What's-his-name had spoken casually and mockingly, his feet propped up on a desk. 'Of course it does, you idiot.'

'Now, now,' said the teacher warningly.

'It's Jupiter, isn't it?' said What's-his-name. 'Then Saturn, Uranus...' No one teased him for saying Uranus. 'Neptune, Earth, Venus, Mars, Mercury and Pluto!'

'Actually, Pluto—' began Simon innocently.

'Pluto, my arse,' said What's-his-name.

'Hey! Boys!'

'You're wrong.' said Simon simply. 'Pluto's a dwarf planet. It doesn't count.'

'Stop contradicting me, idiot. Miss, I'm right, tell him I'm right.'

But, he had been wrong.

And this is why Simon was now shoved up against a sink in the bathroom. The know-it-all kid.

'Are you angry yet, Anderson?'

It was a new voice this time. Simon sighed through gritted teeth. Great, there were two of them.

He didn't recognize this guy. At least the other one looked familiar. This new guy looked about twelve, with a jet-black fringe and deep blue eyes. He was also more fashionable, Simon noted, in jeans, a punk t-shirt, and a silver ring through his nose. He had several leather bracelets around his right wrist.

'No.'

'Why not? I'd be.'

His voice was kind of hypnotic. Simon blinked, several times. The boy who'd just walked in smiled.

'You asked what his name was.' he nodded towards What's-his-name. 'He's James. I'm Alex.'

'Umm... hi Alex?'

'Punch him.' Alex nodded solemnly to James.

Simon barely had time to gasp in surprise before James' fist connected with his face. Simon lurched backwards in shock and hit his head off the mirror, swearing loudly. 'What the hell was that for?'

'Are you frustrated now?'

'Yes!'

'Right. James, shove his head in the toilet.'

'WHAT?'

***

I slipped into the bathroom. It was just as murky and grimy as the restaurant, and small and poky too. There was mould and an unidentified brown substance on the previously (presumably) cream walls. I went into one of the three cubicles. I didn't bother locking or even closing the door. I begin to dial the number into my IPhone. The last number was almost unreadable. It looked like Darrell had wiped something up with it. I pressed the phone to my ear.

And then the bathroom door burst open.

A girl dashed into the bathroom. She was dressed in a waitress' uniform, and although it looked to be a tiny size, it still hung loose on her scrawny, stick-like frame. She had spiky dyed red hair and green, almost cat-like eyes, in which the expression was frantic and frenzied. She dashed straight to the windows over the sink, bashing on the hinges and slamming her fists against the glass. 'Come on!'

'Hey!' I began to emerge from the cubicle. 'Are you—'

'Shut up!' She hissed, spinning around, running her hands through her hair. 'He'll hear!'

The door banged open again, hitting against the wall with a dull thud.

It was not the boy in the doorway I noticed, but the look of pure petrified terror on her face when he entered.

He had had tangled black hair in a fringe and piercing blue eyes, a pale face, jeans and a t-shirt with the name of some band proclaimed across it. He also had a nose piercing. He looked really young, about twelve, but this couldn't be right, as the waitress who was terrified of him looked around seventeen.

'Alright, Jac?' he stared straight through me.

For goodness sake, Trinity, don't be scared of a twelve-year-old boy.

'Hellooooo? Can you see me? Am I invisible to you?'

'You're not, but you're of no interest, so basically as good as,' he said smoothly.

Right, Trinity, you're scared of a twelve-year-old boy.

'What's with your hair? It looks like a bush.'

Personal insults were all I could come up with.

'I know. Please forgive me.' He raised his thin, perfectly-arched eyebrows. 'Now, could you please leave me and Jacqueline in peace? We have some ... personal issues to discuss.'

'No.'

'What?' his smile dropped.

'I'm not taking orders from a twelve-year-old. I don't even know your name!'

'I'm not twelve!'

I realised my phone was still ringing.

***

As James shoved him towards the cubicle, Simon felt his pocket vibrate. This can't be good. And then 'Good Feeling' began to blare out from his phone. James stopped, confused.

'What are you doing, you idiot? Stick his head in the toilet!' groaned Alex.

'You're not the politest, are you?' panted Simon.

'I'm not here to be polite! I'm here to see that this moron knows what he's doing. Which he clearly doesn't.' He glared at James.

'So, what do I—' began James, frowning in concentration.

'Oh, for God's sake, just let him answer it!'

James stood still.

'Let go of his arms!'

He did so. Simon reached into his pocket, and pulled out the phone.

'Hello?' No one answered him.

'Hello?' he said again.

There was a distant mumbling for the other end. He suddenly realized what it was. The person ringing him had not realised he'd picked up the phone. If he concentrated, he could hear the conversation on the other end.

'Who is it?' Alex impatiently interrupted his thoughts.

Simon made a rude gesture at the bully and turned away, shoving his finger in his ear, trying to hear his caller's conversation.

'So what age are you?' came a crackly voice from the other end of the phone. Feminine, Simon thought.

'Sixteen,' came another, a boy's. 'And my name's Alex.'

***

'Hi! Is this Trisha?' Simon sounded excited

'If you mean Trinity, yes it is.' I felt kind of pissed off. He had caught me at a bad time. I was still trying to figure out what was happening between Jacqueline the waitress and this Alex person.

'So... you met Darrell?'

'I did. And I don't see why you couldn't have asked me out yourself!' Alex slipped past me towards Jacqueline. I stepped

70

quickly between them. He may have been a year older, but he was still really short.

'Because... you're posh. And prettier. And richer.'

'I am not posh!'

'Are too!'

This was a bad time to be getting into a fight with someone I'd never met.

'Look, can I call you back later? I have a bit of a situation here, you see ...'

'Is Darrell still there?'

I was kind of taken aback by this. 'Why?'

'I'm in a situation too. As in, about to have my head shoved down a toilet.'

'Oh.'

'Is that all you've got to say?'

'Well, couldn't you call him?'

There were a few moments of silence, then,

'That's not a bad idea, actually.'

'Look, this is a really bad time for me. Some fella called Alex with a really revolting nose piercing is threatening a girl I've never met,'

'Sounds dodgy.'

'It is.'

***

On the other end of the line, Simon was having an epiphany.

'Alex? Did you say Alex? And nose piercing?'

'James! Get the phone!' howled Alex on Simon's side.

'Yeah ... why?' Trinity sounded confused.

71

'What age is he?'

'Well, he says he's sixteen, but he'd barely get into a twelve at the cinema.'

Simon's mouth dropped open. He turns to stare at Alex the bully. The bully with a nose ring who looked about twelve.

'Alex,' he whispered, holding the phone away from his ear. 'What age are you?'

'I'm sixteen.' he growled, grabbing the phone.

'How in the name of God—'

Alex shoved him out of the cubicle, eyes blazing. It was only when the back of his head connected with the wall that he realized he was trapped. Alex's face was inches from his own and Simon could feel his hot, angry breath against his skin.

'Listen to me, Anderson,' Alex hissed through gritted teeth. 'You will keep your nose out of my business, if you know what's good for you. You will leave me and my property alone!'

Now Simon was scared. How could someone be in two places at once? What on earth was going on?

'Got that?'

'I…'

'I said, have you got that!' Alex shook him

'Yeah, yeah!'

'Good.' He gave one last jerk of Simon's collar, then let go of him, dropped his phone in the toilet and flushed it.

'Hey! That's my—'

Alex had the arrogance to turn around and glare at me. 'What?'

'Nothing.'

'Good.'

He turned and left the bathroom with James, who had been silent all this time, following suit. Simon realized with a jolt that James had been what Alex had meant by his 'property'.

How on earth was he meant to phone Darrell now?

***

I stared at the phone in my hand. What had that splashing noise meant? Whatever it was, Simon was scared. Anyway, I had bigger problems to handle. Alex was still trying to push past me. I shielded the cowering Jacqueline.

'Look, whatever the problem is, I'm sure we can solve it in our own good time.'

'This girl belongs to me!' Alex snarled.

'We can all sit down and have a civilised—' I stopped. 'What did you say?'

'She belongs to me! You are preventing me from obtaining my personal property!'

This made me (considering I'd never met this girl in my life) unreasonably angry.

'Look, matey! Slavery was abolished years ago! This girl, and, by the way, she does have a name, belongs to no one, and especially not to you! Have you asked her how she feels about this situation?'

But he didn't get a chance to. We were interrupted, again. This whole situation was getting even more confusing.

Darrell entered the bathroom. When I say entered, blazed is probably a better description. As the bathroom door crashed against the wall, Alex's face turned a distinctly noticeable green.

'Alex! What have I told you, a million times? You've got to keep it secret!'

If I thought he'd been annoyed in the restaurant, it was nothing to how he was acting now. His chest heaved, his breath coming out in gasps. He ran his fingers through his knotted hair in a frenzy.

'Look, Darrell, stay out of this!' Alex yelled straight back. 'You know she's mine! As is James!'

James? Wasn't that the name I'd heard shouted in the background of our phone conversation?

'I only let him get at that Simon guy as reward,' continued Alex, obviously now just as stressed as the rest of us.

'Well, that backfired, didn't it?' shouted Darrell.

'He did what I told him without anything up until now!'

'I'm not yours, you little creep!' hissed Jacqueline from behind me.

'COULD SOMEBODY PLEASE TELL ME WHAT IS GOING ON?'

Alex, Jacqueline and Darrell stopped their bickering and stared at me. Obviously I'd been louder than previously intended.

'Look, Darrell, why are you yelling at Alex? And why is Alex chasing Jacqueline? And why was Simon so scared? What's happening?'

And then, for the third time today, the door slammed against the wall.

'Oh, for goodness' sake,' I groaned.

'Stop slamming the door!' bellowed a voice from the diner.

'Put your hands in the air!'

At the sight of the police officer, Alex made a dash for the same windows Jacqueline had been trying to escape through, and, like her, couldn't get them open. Darrell grabbed the back of his t-shirt and pushed him at the uniformed policeman.

'Darrell! You're my brother! You can't—'

What? Darrell was Alex's brother? They looked totally different!

'Yes I can.' Darrell no longer looked stressed. Just tired. 'Look, Al, I daresay I'll see you later. They'll get you out soon enough.'

These words seemed to subdue Alex. He went quietly with the officer. I turned to Darrell, and was about to demand an explanation when his phone beeped.

He examined the message onscreen.

'It's Simon. He called the police. He'll meet us out front in ten minutes. I'll explain then.'

***

'Alex and I aren't like you, OK?' was the first thing Darrell said, once Jacqueline, Simon and I had gathered around a table. Well, Jacqueline was technically still on waitressing duties. She was just hanging around our table a lot more than the others.

'What?'

'Shut up, Trinity.' Simon elbowed me.

'How dare you! I've only known you ten minutes!'

'Half an hour.'

'Whatever!'

'Shut up, both of you!' Jacqueline elbowed us both. She had very pointy elbows. Pointy enough to quieten the two of us down. 'Carry on, Darrell.'

'We're, well … how do I explain? We have … powers. The general term is "fairies", I suppose, but we're not exactly like fairies. We only have one special power each. Alex's is being in two places at once. Mine is shielding.'

'Shielding?' Simon cut in.

Something strange happened then. I blinked, and when I opened my eyes, Darrell was no longer there. Simon's face stretched into a grin.

'That is so cool!'

'I know, right?' Darrell's voice came from thin air. Then I realised. He was invisible.

'Understand?' he shimmered back into place. 'You can be turned fairy by only one thing. Rain in a fairy circle. You know, those circles of toadstools you get in forests?' he added the last bit for my benefit.

'Looks like they don't teach much nature in posh schools,' sniggered Simon, earning another swift elbow in the side from Jacqueline.

'The process of changing often has some side effects, though. In Alex's case, his extreme possessiveness, or tendency to see other people as belonging to him.'

'That's creepy.' I shuddered.

'I guess,' he shrugged. 'But he's my brother, so I don't really see it as that. Any questions?'

'Uh, yeah.' Jacqueline cut in. 'Darren—'

'Darrell,'

'Sorry, Darrell, when you said to Alex when he was being arrested, "they'll get you out". Who did you mean by that?'

'The Enchantery – that is, the fairy government. They deal with all forms of crime in the fairy world. Unfortunately for Alex, his strange possessiveness is very much against the law.'

'Oh.'

We sat back in silence for a moment, but not for long. Darrell's phone began to buzz again. He groaned as he skimmed the message.

'That was Mr Moran, the police officer. Alex has escaped. He hopped out the back of the van when they stopped in a service station.' He turned to Jacqueline, and said abruptly, 'He'll probably be coming for you. I can count on you to help, yeah, Simon?'

76

I, however, had an issue I needed to address with Simon, and I wasn't waiting until Darrell had finished.

'Yes.'

'What?' he frowned.

'In answer to your earlier question, yes, I will go out with you. Looks like we're going to be seeing rather a lot of each other from now on.'

The Only Option

by Kate Ryan, aged 14

On this window sill of mine,

Legs grown too long this time,

To fit upon the seat,

Where I once watched the sun retreat,

A face easily lined with smiles,

And all just seemed worthwhile.

Eyes no longer spot the wonder

In striking stars, and musical thunder.

The highlight of my life,

Is to sleep through the darkened strife,

No mystery poses the night,

All killed by age's blinding light,

Fairies cannot fly, wings broken,

Bent, left decayed and to weaken

No fluorescent dust left to settle,

Just stung by wide- eyed staring nettles.

Princess dresses cannot fit

Upon these breasts and hips,

The crowns just seem moronic,

Unless worn with a face that's pure ironic.

The prince no longer wants your heart

But hidden skin, shivering and stark,
Yet I still hope to be rescued
From either dragons or the refuse.

A decade and close to a half,
Is all I've got to mock and laugh,
But the dirt has still been sogged,
And the residue stays fogged
Slicked back up on my brain,
Broken by the years of rain,
Just fuzzy little images,
Clouded in an indigo mist,
That I can't tell, bothered to exist.

Just one little attempt,
To squeeze upon the kempt,
Whitewashed, childhood bench,
That only a few years ago,
Used to be my respite,
From divorces and bitter fights,
So I'll pat it tenderly,
And smother it with curtains,
For eternity,

For that's the option left to me.

The Cousins' War

by Ciara Hennessy, aged 15

1

Every woman should marry for her own advantage, since her husband will represent her, as visible as her front door, for the rest of her life. If she chooses a wastrel, she will be avoided by all her neighbours as a poor woman; catch a duke or a marquis and she will be 'Your Grace' and everyone will be her friend. She can be pious, she can be witty, she can be learned and beautiful. But if she is married to a fool she will be 'that poor Mrs Fool' until the day he dies.

Since she was a child of three, Darina St Pol had been betrothed in marriage to Napier Todd, Marquis of Dorset, son of Richard, Earl of Cambridge. Now, at age sixteen, (and he five years her senior), she had to sail to this new country of England from Luxembourg in a beautiful ship with her standard flying high at the top of the mast and be his wife. His country is rich and fertile- filled with fountains and green fields and the sound of dripping water. His country is ripe with warm fruits and scented with flowers. She would be forced to bear the scent of the White York rose instead of the rightful red rose of Lancaster. Her family had always been firmly allied with Lancaster. The sleeping King, Henry VI, was her sister Jaquetta's nephew, and the North strongly supported his wife Margaret of Anjou and her son and heir Edward of Westminster. After Towton, the three sons of York Edward (Plantaganet) of March, Richard (Plantaganet) Duke of Gloucester and George (Plantaganet) Duke of Clarence had taken the country, with Edward on the throne.

She was to be a daughter of Lancaster, but a York wife. She had no choice. Men commanded the world, and some women cannot march to the beat of a man's drum. They make the world their own and everything they learn they claim for themselves. They were like alchemists, who look for the laws that govern the world, and they want to own them and keep them secret. Everything they discover they hug to themselves. They shape knowledge into their own selfish image. What was left to women but the realms of the unknown?

Her mother, Margret de Baux, had always said that women could take their place in the world, if they mind their curses and their words. She did, and Yolande of Aragon did. She was called 'the Queen of Four Kingdoms'.

'Shall I not command great kingdoms like you and her?' A young and breathless Darina had asked once.

'Perhaps.' Her mother had answered gravely, 'but you will be like all women of the world, uneasy in the world of men. You will do your best, but you will always find the road is difficult beneath you. Maybe our ancestress Melusina, the water goddess will hear you?'

Darina hadn't understood then.

2

After three months at the new English court of Edward IV, it was safe to say that the courtesans thought Darina was losing her wits, like the old king. Her eyes flew open and she discovered that she was drenched in sweat. Again. Her healer, an old woman from Wales, had told her that she had 'fuarallas', a condition that affected a minority of young girls, during the warmest months of the year, but she knew better. The Rivers were speaking to her, warning her of danger and forebodings yet to come. She had magic in her blood. Her mother had been right, she was of Melusina's line. She often saw things and made predictions, but magic and witchcraft was forbidden at the court. If she wasn't careful she would be strangled by the blacksmith and buried at the crossroads. Shuddering, she got out of bed, poured herself some small ale and sat down in front of the looking glass.

How different to her sister she was! A smile escaped her. Though both girls were famous beauties, her smoky black hair, milky skin and hazy iris-coloured eyes contrasted startlingly with Jaquetta's cornsilk, straight hair, peach-blossom skin and clear blue eyes. Naturally, her sad and mysterious aura coupled with her striking appearance had attracted many admirers at court, even the king himself (who was famous for have being in half the beds in England), but she always kept them in arm's length with an icy, 'Would you care if I was ugly?' look

A knock on the door brought her back down to earth. She often found that her thoughts were like stars that she could not fathom into constellations. A distraction had arrived in the form of a messenger. She scolded like a shrew. In this country there was no separation between men and women at all. All her ladies had daily callers and stable boys and messengers were always wandering around idly. With a vulgar wink the messenger handed her a piece of parchment and departed. She recognised the elegant script writing immediately. Years of forced correspondence overseas from her tutor meant that she recognised Napier Todd's personal hand anywhere. A letter from him was very unusual. They had lost contact before Towton, which was two years ago. As she read the letter, her heart rate increased. It seemed Richard Neville; Earl of Warwick had convinced Edward to grant their marriage proposal in celebration of the peace treaty between England and France, and his betrothal to Princess Bona. She was to be married! Today! With no friends or family, or even her father or brother to give her away! She hadn't even met Napier yet! The standard procedure was a month of public courting before marriage. To say that she had butterflies in her stomach would be an underestimate, as dragons were flying around, snapping viciously and breathing fire.

Her ladies hurried in, all in a dither and began to get her ready for her formal presentation to Napier. From what she could make out, Napier was legendary on the battlefield and much adored by all the ladies at court. The whisper of the Rivers in her head had started again, but the words were slurred and hoarse. She found she had a splitting headache in a matter of minutes. All she could do was squeeze her eyes shut and let them dress her. When she dared to peek, she was quickly lost for words.

3

The girl in the looking glass was a haunting and unearthly beauty. She looked like a flower, or a girl made from flowers. The plush velvet of the dark green, almost black, velvet of the dress set off her ivory completion and tumbling ebony curls. The bodice, embodied with thousands of twinkling crystals, stretched from collarbone to naval, revealing a generous amount of cleavage, but stopped short of anything obscene. Her hair was fashionable arranged and plucked at the forehead, which emphasised her dark eyes and featherlike eyelashes. For a moment she had thought that Melusina had appeared to her.

Noon found Darina waiting uneasily in the courtyard. In the distance she could hear the joyous crowds cheering, singing, clapping and dancing. The minutes dragged by slowly until the noise grew into a crescendo and the portcullis swung down. One by one, white rose clad soldiers marched in, each turning their heads respectfully to the Neville's, Duchess Cecily, King Edward, Richard and George. Finally, a majestic figure on a proud warhorse trotted in, and with a graceful salute, Napier swing out of the saddle. Darina held her breath, as he reached up to take his helmet off.

The man under the helmet was so dashingly beautiful that he was almost painful to look at. He had the face of a Greek God. His sharp cheekbones, proud brow and straight aristocratic nose made him a sculptures dream. When he smiled, a dimple appeared, beneath his chin, giving him a slightly mischievous look and when he moved, he was so graceful and lithe that he made the simple move look like a dance. Light danced off his honeycomb hair, casting half his face in a shadow. When his eyes, a stormy grey that were alternately thoughtful and intense found hers, she felt a fierce and wonderful thing in the core of her being.

It was by far the most intense thing she had ever experienced. She gasped again, seeing stars. A pure line of communication had been opened between them; it was a fierce and terrible thing, a bit like being fused together by a bolt of lightning. But it was also so wonderful that her entire skin was prickling and her mind was blissfully hushed with awe. She felt as if she had been lifted into some new and wonderful place that most people never saw. The air around them seemed to quiver with tiny invisible wings. 'I love you' she thought, looking at him. 'I love every part of you, every thought and word ... the entire complex, fascinating bundle of all the things you are. I want you with ten different kinds of need at once. I love all the seasons of you, the way you are now, the thought of how much more beautiful you'll be in the decades to come. I love you for being the answer to every question my heart could ask.'

'Cara, Semper,' he whispered, as his lips brushed her hand. The spot where they had met her skin burned deliciously. Her mother had always taught her to keep her eyes modestly to the ground, but she could not help but stare.

Darina was torn away unwillingly to prepare for the wedding. Serene in its simplicity, her gown felt like nothing on its hanger and a whisper between her fingers. It hung elegantly on her birdlike figure, making her look like a misguided angel.

4

They were married within the hour, and the banquet flowed smoothly into the hall as a result of flawless planning. The finest sweetmeats, almonds soaked in summer fruits and pastries were served and there was dancing long into the night, though Darina preferred the country dances from her childhood in Luxembourg. Napier held her for the whole night and eventually they were able to slip out into the cool night to walk across the battlements to admire the view of the river. The voices in her head were screaming to protest, but they were easily ignored.

As they walked, Napier pulled Darina closer. Her young, childlike physique seemed to fit perfectly into his broad, battle-hardened body. Their immodesty that should have made her blush and protest made her dizzy and merry with joy. With a quick and definite motion, Napier swung her around so that she was facing the rising moon. Then he reached into his tunic and produced a small ornately carved ancient wooden box, inlaid with gold and mother-of-pearl. It was ornamented with a rainbow of gemstones. The box itself was a priceless treasure, and it would have outshone just about any piece of jewellery besides the one inside it. The necklace, artfully arranged in red velvet, was simple gold-woven into a thick rope of a chain, almost scaled. It was like a smooth serpent that would curl and close around the throat. One jewel hung suspended from the rope- a white diamond.

'This is for you, to match your beauty,' Napier smiled shyly 'I used to think that Helen of Troy was the most beautiful woman that ever existed, but now I know that Helen has been eclipsed.'

'I should be afraid to touch it,' she whispered

Napier tied the necklace around her swanlike neck, then spoke:

'I want you cool and regal, earthy and impertinent, spoiling for a fight and abashed at your own temper. I want you flushed with exertion and rosy with sleep. I want you teasing and provocative, sombre and thoughtful. I want every emotion, every mood, every year in a lifetime to come. I want you beside me, to encourage and argue with me, to help me and let me help you. I want to be your champion and lover, your mentor and student, because I love you more than my own life.'

Darina's entire anatomy swelled with joy.

They conversed for a while in Latin, until Darina noticed some ravishing water lilies growing by the riverbank. Filled with longing for anything connected to the river, she sweetly asked Napier to pick them for her. Just as he started to leave, a nearby foot soldier hurried over eagerly and offered to pick them for her instead (he had long since nursed a soft spot for Darina)

While the enthusiastic foot soldier was retrieving them, Napier, who was eager to impress, stood watch.

'ARRRGHH!!'

Darina snapped out of her daydream as she heard a drunken grunt and a soft thud. Her blood ran cold as she edged cautiously around the corner. John Beaufort, Duke of Somerset was plainly in view muttering to himself, as he wiped his dagger in his trousers. He swayed slightly as he squinted and recognised her

5

'That lazy good-for-nothing soldier was sleeping on his watch,' he explained gruffly. 'Don't worry, I took good care of it'

As he stumbled past her, she was hit by wave of strong ale and male odour that made her gag. She noticed a sticky crimson substance on the palms of his hands and in the deep crescents of his fingernails. Her breathing increased as she edged towards the dead soldier. As she recognised him, she felt an agonising tearing sensation in her chest. She knew her heart was broken. It was Napier. Napier, who was supposed to die in her bed beside her. Her Napier, who had all but walked through hell on the battlefield and learned the devils name to find her. Her strong, handsome, clever husband, killed in a dream by a drunken traitor of York and Lancaster. She shrieked and wailed and created salt beads with melting eyes. She shouted in gibberish as she clung to his chest and breathed in his familiar scent of rose-clear water and leather.

She lay there, for hours, suffocating under the weight of her loss, until her mind sharpened. She could faintly hear the eerie sweet whisper of the River's song. When a daughter of Melusina was dying, her Rivers sang to welcome her and guide her into the next world. With a burst of illuminating white light, Darina had a vision. She was in a dark clearing, surrounded by a tangle of dense trees. In the centre, there was a woman, an alluring and enticing woman with snowy white skin and heavy dark hair bathing in a marble pool. Instinct told Darina that it was Melusina, but she had Darina's face. There was a slight rustling behind her and Napier appeared, and smiled as her opened his arms to embrace her. Soulmates! Like Melusina and the knight. The Soulmate Principle was the idea of two people being destined for each other at birth. Usually, the soulmates provide each other with understanding, healing and strength. It meant that there's only one love for everyone who exists. And when you meet that love, you know them. You know you were meant to be together, and nothing can keep you apart, not even death itself. No matter what else goes wrong, with that one person they'd be safe in their own paradise.

Suddenly, Darina was filled with courage and certainty. She stood up and made her way to the river.

She waded out until her head was completely submerged. As the current pulled her along she crashed into a rock, but it was just a little splash of rain. Nothing could hurt her now.

'Melusina, Mother of the water, receive my soul and return me to my love,' she thought as she fell asleep.

Summer

by Saoirse Duignan, aged 13

The ivy wrapped around,
The long branch,
Stretched from Mother Nature's arms,
Wrapping, strangling the tree in its grasp.

Summer is when misery comes,
When you have no friends to talk to,
It goes in a blink of an eye,
When you wish it would end,
The days seem longer,
At the end you wonder,
Did you really count the days off?
Why couldn't have counted,
The moments with the air rushing past you,
Why couldn't you have made friends
With the people who were willing to be your friend?
Why could you not have made that summer last?

The pen and the ink, seem like tools for destruction,
Books seem so alien like, the words jump out and eat you,
Your school uniform seems so tight and heavy,
It seems to be like they were glued on,
On that first day back at school.

Success

by Patrick Sweeney, aged 15

As I look down at her frail, beaten corpse, I think to myself 'Success!' But was it worth it? After all the planning, all the virtual 'small talk', is the success not bittersweet? She was only seventeen. I had my fun, but at the cost of an innocent girl's life. What has become of me? Where did I go wrong...?

When I woke early yesterday morning to the sound of the skylark singing, I knew I was ready. I opened my curtains and looked outside. The dew of the morn covered the grass like a thick blanket covering the harshness of the world. It had been three months now and Jenny and Mike were really close friends. She was so flawless in her profile picture on Facebook. Her long, blonde, wavy hair lay gently on her shoulders and she was dressed in a short red dress, which complemented her big, blue eyes. Perfection. She was so open with Mike. We had learned so much about her in the last couple of months. Her profile wasn't private so finding out all about her casual, laidback lifestyle was not a tedious task. She continued to flirt with Mike, complementing him on his strong masculine build and his dreamy brown eyes. But as I got ready to meet Jenny for the first time on that warm summer's day, I saw the real Mike staring back at me, nervous in the mirror. How would Jenny react when she realised her strong, seventeen-year-old Dublin 'Hottie' was actually a fifty-nine-year-old, lonely man who would sit through the night staring at her hourglass figure within his own computer screen.

Mike had arranged to meet Jenny inside Starbucks for a coffee and a chance to finally expand their relationship status on Facebook from 'friends' to 'in a relationship'. I sat down with a coffee and waited. I was nervous now, but at the same time excited. This was it. The day in my life when things finally started to get better for me. I would no longer be the lonely old creep who stared at the young adults as they left the school grounds. Today I would find my soul mate and there would be no need for

Mike anymore. As Jenny walked in the world seemed to freeze around me. She was wearing a bright blue hoodie over a purple lace top. The same top she had on in one of her 'mobile uploads' on her timeline. Her small red skirt was just above knee length and I figured she must be cold. Would she take my old leather coat for the journey home to my house?

I watched her touch up her makeup and I started to feel good about myself as I thought, 'This is all for me!' I combed back my grey, greasy hair and made my move. As I approached, Jenny continued to apply her lipstick and she didn't notice me coming until I was standing, breathing over her shoulder.

'Is someone sitting here?' I croaked.

She jumped and stared at me in surprise. I smiled at her. She was so beautiful in real life. So much more than a photo or a 'hey' in chat. My palms turned sweaty as I waited for a reply. 'Em, sorry my friend Mike is coming in a …'

'Mike?' I interrupted. 'The seventeen-year-old brown-haired boy whose computer won't let him upload anymore photos of himself?' This scared her. You could see the colour drain from her face. She stared back at me as I sat down. I grabbed her small shaking hand quickly so she could not pull away. 'It's me…I'm Mike!' I felt relieved as I said it. My secret was out, no more hiding.

She didn't jump or open her mouth in disbelief. She didn't embrace me either like I thought she would. For the few seconds it took for her brain to work out what was going on, we sat in silence. Together. I finally felt that someone was there for me. All the work had paid off and I was finally going to be with Jenny. Success! She was mine. Or at least I thought she was...

'You sick pathetic, old loner! You're nothing but a paedophile! ROT IN HELL!' I sat in utter confusion for a moment as she stormed out of the shop, tears streaming down her face. What had just happened? It was going so well. How could Jenny just leave me? She couldn't. I wouldn't let her. All the hours spent on the computer weren't for nothing. Jenny was coming home with me tonight no matter what it took. My shock turned to rage as I ran out of the shop. I could see her wiping her eyes across the road talking to herself. She looked a mess. I saw a small stout guard getting out of his car near me. He had also noticed Jenny and he seemed concerned. I had to act quickly or my dream would be snatched away from me right before my eyes.

I shouted at him, 'Please! Stop my daughter! She's had too much to drink and won't come back!' He nodded his brainless head and went to Jenny. I had her now. I went and got my car and pulled round to Jenny and the guard. 'Thank you so much officer, I was so worried she'd slip away from me...'

Jenny went pale when she realised what was happening. Terror caused her to freeze and I acted quickly when she was in this state of disbelief. As I began to push her into the car, Jenny went hysterical. The guard left me to deal with her, oblivious to the fact that this was a kidnapping and that tonight when I was finished with her, Jenny would be nothing but a beaten corpse sprawled out in the bedroom. One hit with the crow bar and Jenny lay asleep in the back seats. She still looked beautiful with her makeup smudged by her tears. 'We will be happy together,' I said. 'Just like we planned on Facebook'...

Now, as I step back and see the damage and pain I have inflicted on this young girl, I think to myself 'Success!' But was it worth it? After all the planning, all the virtual 'small talk' and at the cost of a life, is the success not bittersweet? Jenny may be gone now, but Mike lives on, ready and waiting. There are plenty more fish in the sea and with the help of Facebook, I won't be long waiting for my next victim...

One in the Chamber

by Pierce O'Brien, aged 17

It took a lot of courage to get into Syria, now I was regretting it. I sat in the back of a truck. A black, heavy bag covering my head. A string tied around the bottom of it and around my neck to keep me from shaking it off. My breathing hot and moist from wearing the bag was shallow and presumably very loud. I shake my head in an attempt to get rid of the bag. As I do, I hear heavy boots, hit the floor of the truck and approach. Something hits me hard at my jaw and again I am knocked out.

'Hey, wakey, wakey.' I open my eyes to a dimly lit figure in front of me. It takes a couple of seconds for my vision to focus but when it does I am met with skinny, average height, bronze colour skinned man that could be no older than twenty one. I quickly look around to see two other men of around the same age. One with practically no hair and a lot of acne scars, the other with a beard and sideburns that just can't quite seem to reach the beard. Behind them I see five other people, all with the same bags on their head I had sitting on the floor. All looking around underneath their bags, blind to their surroundings and clearly clueless as to what is going on. I glance around me once more to see I am in a small, dimly lit warehouse. I look back to the man in front of me as he acknowledges I am ready to listen.

'So, my friend, here is what is going to happen,' he says grinning wildly with excitement 'We have taken you and your silly little news team and have brought you here to play a game to stop you broadcasting these terrible things you do about our people. If the game goes well for you, you leave safely and will have hopefully learnt your lesson. However, if it does not, you will die.' He finishes his sentence and stops for a minute to let out an excited little giggle. 'Okay, okay, so first you must decide if you want to play the game!' As he says this he takes out two handguns out of his back pocket. One M1911 pistol, the other a .44 magnum revolver. 'Okay, so you must choose, if you would like to play the game. If you choose the pistol you refuse to play the game, I take it and shoot all of your news team in the head and you walk free. If you choose the revolver, you put your life on the line and your news team go free'. Now realising my hands and legs are still bound to the chair I am in, he comes around and unties my left hand gesturing for me to choose. I swallow, horrified at my choice and look up at him.

'How do I know you won't just kill us all regardless of my choice?' I ask, my voice shaking with terror.

'You don't!' he says and leans back with an explosion of laughter.

Looking around, terrified, I look back to the two guns now at the table in front of me and point my hand at the revolver.

'Fantastic choice!' he says with wide eyes as he excitedly tosses the handgun to his man by my news team. The henchman raises the gun and quickly unloads all five bullets into the wall. With a quiet sigh of relief I turn to him so he can explain what comes next.

'So now,' he says picking up the revolver, 'we are going to play a game I am sure you have heard of called Russian roulette' he says as he flicks the barrel open and shows me the one bullet amongst the six chambers. 'Each of us will take turns putting the barrel into our mouths and pulling the trigger!' he yells excitedly. Spinning the barrel with his palm, he flicks the revolver shut so neither of us see which chamber the bullet is in. He takes the revolver and places it on its side on the table. Placing his fingers on the butt of it he gives it a gentle push so it spins on the table. It spins five times before it gently glides to a halt, with the barrel facing me. I look up to find him smiling sadistically at me, 'Looks like you'll be going first, my friend'.

I wrap my hand around the revolver and pick it up slowly. It's very heavy in my hand, much heavier than I expected. I pull the hammer back to a great resistance; eventually it clicks back into place. My hand shaking, places the revolver in my mouth. I scream and pull the trigger. The hammer clicks back into place. I throw

the gun back on the table and breathe a sigh of relief. He steps up
to the table now; he picks up the gun with a smirk on his face.
'How about we change the rules of the game around' he says. 'I'm
notoriously lucky in this game, and want to give you a chance by
favouring your odds. How about I take the next four shots and if I
survive you take the last?' Shaking in my seat from the adrenaline I
apprehensively nod.

He picks the gun up and it seems light in his hand. He leans
forward, bending over the table and sticks his free hand, his left,
out to the side. Now he is bent over the table, gun in his mouth
with this other arm outstretched. He looks similar to a magician
about to perform a magic trick. If he pulls this off without blowing
his brains out he must be one. He cocks the hammer of the
revolver using his thumb with ease. He stares me straight in the
eye.

Click

Cocks the hammer

Click

Cocks the hammer

BANG

I flinch so violently back into my chair it almost topples back.
When I land forward and open my eyes, the man who seconds ago
was smirking sadistically at me now lies dead under the table with
a hole the size of a fist in the back of his head. His henchmen stare
wide-eyed clearly unprepared for this. Suddenly one makes a move
for me across the room, the other for my news team. Both pull out
hunter's knives and the one with the bad acne scars goes behind
me and cuts my ties. The other does the same to my news team
and we somehow stand up all shaking. The one with the acne
scars looks at us all

'Congratulations, you win, now go.'

Brave Little Bird

by Michelle Helena Monaghan, aged 18

I'm sitting at my window. The sky is getting dark,

I'm looking at my reflection but I can't see the spark

That everyone else seems to see when the sky is bright

But with the sun the spark goes out like an artificial light.

My eyes now are solemn and alone,

I can't remember the last time they had tone.

I'm sitting at my window. Now the stars are coming out.

All the emotions inside me are making me want to shout.

But still I hold it in, still I try to be brave

Because sooner or later I'll find the light at the end of the cave.

I'm sitting at my window, the moon's now in the sky.

I'm looking at a landed bird getting ready to fly.

But before the bird spreads its wings a cat pulls it down.

Watching this I let a sigh and my face goes to a frown.

But still the bird it struggles, hoping to get free.

With one great tug it loses grip and soars up in the air with glee.

Although the bird is injured, it still keeps flapping on,

It reminded me of courage, something so small being so strong.

I'm sitting at my window, I'm thinking of the Earth,

How the little bird continued on, even though it was hurt.

I get up from my window, my reflection turns away.

An unfamiliar smile appears on my face at the start of a new day.

The bird gives you wonder, the bird gives you song,

But to me the bird gave courage, and showed me how to be strong.

The Bazaar That Betrayed a Secret

by Kathryn Keane, aged 17

As Tiernan passes through the gates and under the sign saying, 'Bizarre Bazaar: Open until the Music Stops', he brushes his cane in a wide arc around him. People openly throw him pitying glances – he's supposedly blind, after all. He ducks his head. He hates this part of pretending. Then the horde parts, allowing him through. He's relieved: besides escaping being elbowed in the ribs and squashed between pickpockets and perverts like everyone else, he can avoid small talk with strangers. Guilt stirs awake again, though. He will never deserve any special treatment, let alone special blind-guy treatment.

He treads uncertainly inward. He cocks an ear. Although no speakers or musicians are visible anywhere, a high, haunting melody spirals around the inside of the Bazaar. It's just audible over the clashing of a thousand different voices. Behind his dark glasses, Tiernan's eyes flicker around the scene.

Rickety little stalls squeeze beside silken, striped pavilions. No order is evident in their placement – the tents and marquees and endless shelves are shoved wherever there's room. A roar comes from a nearby knot of people. On a raised platform before them, a giant white rabbit holds a top hat out and pulls a terrified-looking man from its depths. Tiernan winces in sympathy but hurries on.

It's hard to make out exact features through twilight's blanket, yet cold goose bumps scurry up Tiernan's arms whenever he looks at the sellers. Maybe it's the gleaming of their eyes. Maybe it's the shimmer of their skin. Maybe it's the fact that the more he stares, the less human their faces look. Sometimes, when he glimpses them out of the corner of his eye, he could swear they have no faces at all.

Maybe that's not their fault, though. As Tiernan slips past a marquee bursting with jaguars and leopards, he happens upon a stall selling various visual aids. He tries to ignore the seller's staring eyes – all forty-eight of them.

'If I know anything well, I know eyes,' she booms, making him jump, 'and I'd have to be blind to think you are.' Her eyes linger on him, just for a moment.

He blinks. 'H-how did you know?' He draws closer – is it obvious to everyone?

'Sorry, that's a trade secret, pet.' She gives him the kindly, slightly patronising smile he seems to get from all women, including the ones he has tried to take home. He has never understood it. He has a feeling he doesn't want to. 'But I've got something new in I think you might like.' She rummages in the counter below and brings out an armful of boxes. 'It's called the EyeGuise. It'll convincingly make your eyes look any colour and shape you want.'

'Can I try a pair on?'

'Of course. I've got a few sample pairs here.' She bends over again to get them. Just as she places them on the counter and Tiernan takes one, he spots Steph striding in their direction.

Tiernan's colleague Steph has wafting, blonde, straightened hair and has never to his knowledge worn a skirt that ends below the knee. When she smiles, he wishes it was at him. When she crosses and uncrosses her long, slim legs, he stares, and swallows, then buries himself in mounds of work. Her expensive sunglasses serve as a permanent barrier. She's taller than him, although it's probably just her high heels. Probably. Tiernan mutters some excuse about seeing his reflection with the EyeGuise on, then ducks around the display to the left and ends up in front of the mirror.

They look exactly like ordinary glasses. Their lenses are even clear. He leaves his cane leaning against the display. Dropping his own dark glasses onto the stall, he hesitantly unfolds the lime green frames and places them over his nose. Nothing happens. Then he whispers, 'Brown, almond-shaped. Please.' The glass shimmers and changes – until it looks exactly as if his eyes are brown and almond-shaped. The illusion blinks and moves in perfect time with his real eyes. It even shines a little too brightly, and blinks, hurriedly.

Tiernan gulps and looks up to find that Steph has arrived at the stall. He hides himself a little more thoroughly behind the display, but can't quite stop himself from letting his gaze linger on her and eavesdropping on her conversation with the seller.

'So these actually do disguise your eyes?' Steph says, picking up one of the sample pairs of EyeGuises.

'It's a lifetime guarantee at a very reasonable price,' replies the seller.

Surprise rises onto Steph's face, but it fast vanishes. 'Oh, that's strange. Because where did I see them before? I think I remember – inside a party bag when I was five.'

'I can assure you that you didn't.' The seller folds her arms in front of her chest.

'How much?' Steph asks abruptly.

'Forty-five euro a pair.'

'That dear? No wonder you haven't sold any.'

'Fine. How about forty?'

'Try thirty-five and I might consider buying.'

'You know, I'd love to discuss this all night,' says the seller, glaring with all her eyes that face Steph.

'But I'm swapping places with someone else soon. And this is the Bazaar's last night here. And,' Tiernan starts as three of the seller's eyes zone in on him, 'there are other customers who haven't paid yet, who would be very unfortunate if they had to test my security.'

'Can I try a pair on, then?' Steph requests. Her long, manicured nails tap out an uneven rhythm on the counter. She reaches up with her other hand to tug and twist a lock of her hair.

The seller nods. Steph looks over both shoulders, ducks her head, and snatches off her sunglasses. Tiernan takes one look at her eyes and gasps.

Steph has owls' eyes.

Yellow, like pools of liquid gold, they almost glow in the rapidly approaching night. Steph shoves on the EyeGuise and activates it immediately, but her real eyes shine on in Tiernan's head. She moves towards the mirror.

'Hurry up!' calls the seller. Turning away, Tiernan tries to go around the back of the stall to pay. It's too late.

'Tiernan?' says Steph, giving him what appears to be a slightly condescending look. In response, Tiernan does a perfect imitation of a goldfish. It's just a pity that everything goes black in the middle of it.

Tiernan rips off the EyeGuise and claps his hands to his eyes. His eye sockets feel hollow. Tentatively he opens his eyelids and places his index fingers into the sockets. They're empty. He slowly slides the EyeGuise back on.

'S-Steph?' he asks. 'Have you gone blind too?'

'Yes,' she answers. 'Hang on – how did you know?'

'I have too. Just now.'

'Were you not blind before?'

Oh God, he completely forgot. 'I– I–'

'Faking a disability to get the good parking spaces first? Didn't think you had it in you.' Surprisingly, her tone is laced with a distracted kind of amusement.

Well, if she's come up with a plausible reason for it independently, he's not going to argue with it. Tiernan makes to lean against where he remembers the counter of the stall to be. His hand hits something made of glass. As he paws blindly around, he knocks it over with a thud.

'Sorry,' he mumbles, scared.

'Idiot!' an unfamiliar Scottish accent snarls. A hand presses itself against his chest and shoves him backwards. 'I spent ten months bottling that starlight before you blundered over here!'

'What? Where's the glasses stall?'

'It's swapped places,' says Steph. 'Remember what she said?'

'So how do we find her and get our sight back?' Tiernan says faintly. 'I didn't see anyone else knowing things about eyes around here...'

'We? You go and look for her if you want, but I'm leaving.'

A cool gust sweeps through the Bazaar. 'But you've gone blind.'

'I don't really care.'

His stomach churns like a washing machine. 'You don't have to go that far to hide your eyes, you know.'

'What do you mean?' Her voice sharpens enough to cut diamonds.

'I saw your owls' eyes,' Tiernan says quietly. 'And I don't mind.'

Silence stretches between them. Has Steph left? Tiernan thinks she has, until he jumps. Steph howls with the kind of laughter so unrestrained and alarming it's mirthless. He wishes he could back away a little, but he'd never find her again.

'You know,' she breathes, 'I think I like you, Tiernan. Maybe I will come along for the ride.'

As she says this, Tiernan notices something. 'We'll have to hurry up,' he tells her. 'The Bazaar moves on when the music stops, and it's already really quiet.'

Steph's footsteps move to his right side. Steph's hand grips his limp one, and the feel of those fingers entwined with his own and their palms tightly pressed together makes Tiernan swallow and take a breath at this almost-an-intimacy. Her warm breath coats his ear. 'So let's run.'

And they do. She elbows people out of the way with her free arm while he shouts, 'Sorry!' as he's dragged past them. He yells, 'Has anyone seen the glasses stall?' over the crowd with less abandon than he's ever had. She calls too, cries, 'the glasses stall? Where's the glasses stall?' Abuse, curses and shouts of pain follow them as they stumble sightless through the pressing crowd, but they don't look back. They can't.

Now they seem to have an easier time getting through. The crowd becomes more widely spaced, but dread pools in Tiernan – that means they're leaving. The music dips lower still; when they shout, they can no longer hear it. His pulse drums louder in his ears than anything else. Puffs for air punctuate Steph's calls.

'Can we stop for a minute?' she finally asks. 'I don't think I can run for much longer.'

'Okay.' Neither can Tiernan. Steph loosens her hold on his hand and breathes out. Automatically, he tries to look at her, then moves his head back. His words stick like congealing honey in his throat.

'When you get your eyes back,' Tiernan says slowly, 'will you hide them again?'

'I'll have to. Nobody will go near me otherwise.' Her voice is flat. 'I don't blame them. After all, I'm a freak.'

'You're not a freak.' And for the first time in his life, Tiernan actually believes himself.

He senses from Steph's tone that she smiles a little as she speaks again. 'If you say so, Tiernan. If you say so.'

Clearing his throat, he says, 'Right – so – will we get going again?'

They run on. 'Has anyone seen the glasses stall?' Steph calls out. Nobody answers. The music has become so quiet it can barely be heard at all.

'The glasses stall? Where's the glasses stall?' Tiernan's voice quivers at the end of the question.

'OVER HERE!' comes a distant shout – the seller's voice.

'Thank God,' whispers Steph, then, louder, 'Where are you?'

'Go right!' comes the reply, and they quickly obey. 'Okay, keep going – a bit to the left, left, I said! That's right, now, go straight ahead, yes, come on – and you're HERE!'

Tiernan's hip bangs painfully into the stall, but he couldn't care less. Steph, just behind, lets go of his hand.

'Listen,' says Steph, 'when you swapped places our eyes completely disappeared. Do you have any idea why it happened or how we can get them back or—'

'Sorry,' the seller cuts in, 'that was a security precaution. All you have to do is take off the EyeGuises and put them on this stall.'

Tiernan gulps. How is he going to do this in front of Steph? He closes his eyes, slides the EyeGuise off his nose and places it back on the stall. The music goes silent. The Bizarre Bazaar has moved on; now it's just him and Steph alone in a field.

'Why haven't you opened your eyes?' she demands. 'Is there something wrong?'

Adrenaline sears through him. Will she mind? What will she say? Yet there's no other option, not as far as he can see.

Tiernan takes a deep breath and opens his eyes.

His yellow, round, glowing owl eyes.

The Fighter

by Gráinne Hamill, aged 16

His heart pumped in his chest as he made his way into the ring, the shouts and cheers went right over his head, as he tried to run through his plan for the hundredth time that day.

Her body shook as she watched him make his way into the ring, she had never felt such fear for another person in her life and she hated to admit it but she kind of loved the feeling. The feeling of caring. God, she was falling in love with The Fighter.

Before stepping into the ring he quickly scanned the crowd for her face and a smile broke across his as he spotted her. She had shown up. Her lip was caught between her teeth and she was shaking. Fear was running through her eyes and he promised himself in that moment he'd fight well tonight, prove to her he'd be okay. They'd be okay.

She saw his breath-taking green eyes reach hers and she prayed he wouldn't understand the emotion that was running through them, but as a look of concentration crossed his features, she knew that he knew. He was going to prove her wrong, she could tell in the way he took his first step into the ring.

As the match began, he was determined to prove her wrong and she was afraid for his safety.

He protected himself well, keeping his guard tight as his opponent took hit after hit. He always did this in the first round. He'd try to wear his competition out before round two and that was when he'd start to get some points on the board. He knew how to play this game, it was like life. You let it try and get you down, but it always fails and when everyone least expects it; you bounce back with a hard jab to the face.

His opponent was a big fellow, he had arms the size of her head and he would have towered over her. She didn't understand what he was doing; he was letting his opponent take hit after hit and not even trying to fight it. God if he didn't get himself killed, she was going to have to do it. After of course she kissed him and told him exactly how she felt.

Round 2 began and he could see the look of tiredness already on his opponent's face. He'd have him in this round that was for sure, but round 3 was going to be hard. He'd have to fight with his life to win. His opponent wasn't expecting him to fight in this round, but he was going to show him exactly why you shouldn't let your guard down. Not now, not ever.

He began the round well, falling into a smooth dance around his opponent and she could tell he had this. His jab came out again and again, hitting him nearly every time. His opponent didn't have a very good guard. As his fist came up underneath to hit his opponent in the stomach she knew it was going to end badly. His opponent read his move and blocked him, but also took advantage of his guard being down.

His opponent's fist came out so fast The Fighter had no way to protect himself, but somehow he ducked just in time and his opponent missed by inches; hitting nothing but air. His fist came up and hit his opponent full force in the jaw, his head snapping back and a groan escaping his lips.

He quickly jumped out of the way before his opponent recovered. She was proud of him he was doing well, he wasn't letting life get at him, but his opponent was going to get him back for that as soon as round 3 began and her heart ached at the thought of him getting hurt.

Round 3 had begun, and a few seconds in, pain had shot through his body with a hit his opponent had thrown at him. He had to get his mind back in the game or he was screwed.

The fear running in her veins had suddenly disappeared as she ran forward, towards the ring. Screaming his name and telling him exactly what he needed to do, to win.

He heard her sweet voice, the voice that he had awoken to, fallen asleep to. It was the voice that kept him sane, shouting instructions at him. The fighter inside her had come out to help him.

She knew he could hear her and the bundle of nerves subsided within her. He'd be okay, and she'd be okay. They'd get through all this. The fight, the hardships in life because they had each other. They were fighters, and they always would be.

As the final bell rang out, they both smiled in unison. They had won this. The first battle, at least.

Art

by Ríona Burke, aged 17

I never considered that there was anything wrong with me, or my life. I was your average student. Wake up, eat breakfast, go to school, complain about school, go home, complain about homework, do homework then work on my projects. Standard seventeen-year-old's existence right?

I suppose I was slightly different than my peers in a few aspects, I never cared much for 'societal norms', I shunned social situations and I avoided sports like the plague. Oh. I also had a healthy appreciation for art.

For as long as I could remember I saw everything in a strange way. No-one else could see the beauty in certain objects, a strand of hair as it fell across a face due to a draught and lay there glowing copper in the sunset, a rivulet of blood hanging suspended for a brief moment in time before it falling leaving a scarlet circlet on the floor, the thin blade of a scalpel shining silver under the glare of industrial lighting. All of these things and more were the most beautiful things I could see. Everybody scorned me for it; I guess their boring, superficial lives were incapable of providing the wonder needed for such images. Of course I didn't voice this out loud, no, I was far too shy, so I contented myself in the way of all quiet people and said it my head with biting sarcasm and as much derision as possible while outwardly I shrugged and smiled. No-one suspects you and that's fine with me.

My silence and general dislike of my peers had another unintended but completely welcomed side effect. To all but a select few, I was effectively invisible. Even my parents forgot I was there half the time and I wouldn't have it any other way. Oh sure, most others crave parental love and acceptance but I was fine without it. My parents extended it to my model older sister. She had a social life, a boyfriend and good grades. I was the weird one who sat in my room drawing or writing or something, with no friends and certainly no boyfriend although I suppose I wouldn't mind one if one was offered. No I preferred my art by far. There's something so satisfying about seeing simple lines come together to create something beautiful. Faces, plants, food, animals. It doesn't really matter. It's all beautiful to me. Judging by the media attention it sometimes gets, I suppose my art is beautiful to others as well. I hope there's someone out there who sees it and appreciates the effort I put in. Weeks and weeks of work and careful notes, the often-physical aspect, the solitude needed. It's surprisingly hard to find a quiet area in the suburbs you know. I like to think that someone out there will see me for who I am and how it reflects in my work and perhaps if I'm lucky I'll inspire them and create a fellow artist just like me.

Speaking of work, the research on my latest project was finally done. This was a long one. I devoted every spare hour to it, committing everything to memory and then transferring what I'd learned to a sheet of paper so as to keep track and dispose of information easily should anything go wrong. I spent so long on this one that my parents actually noted my absence and confronted me about it. I told them that everything was fine and that I'd decided to try and take up walking. They believed me, surprisingly. I suppose the old trick of mixing truth in with a lie to give it substance actually works and in fairness I did spend a lot of time walking, just not with the aim to keep fit, they jumped to that conclusion themselves. For once I was actually thankful that I was surrounded by such mundane minds. It made things easier for me.

The convenient explanation for my absence satisfied them and I quickly faded back into obscurity thankfully. Too much longer and my project would fail.

I left the house that night using the excuse I reserved exclusively for times like these. Camping. It was a solitary activity so I had no need to endure friends in order to provide an alibi. It was a clear night too, cold and fresh. The sky was huge and hung heavy with stars, perfect for the final stage of my project.

I hiked to the top of the scrubland out by the old abandoned warehouse. It was quite a journey and very secluded. Any road there might have been was gone and most people had forgotten about it. I got there and pitched my tent so it wasn't immediately noticeable. I rolled out my sleeping bag, unpacked the food and set up camp, and then I settled in to wait.

An owl hooted and the trees rustled in the slight breeze. All around me, house lights went off one by one until it was just me and the stars. I checked the time on my phone. Five minutes. I was getting twitchy now, fingers itching with a desire to draw, to trace, to create my masterpiece. Four minutes. Three. Two. Finally, the swishing of grass, the heavy tread of boot-clad feet. My research had paid off. Here came my centrepiece right on time.

He stumbled into my camp and looked round in surprise. I put my acting skills to good use and looked the very picture of a startled teen. I offered him coffee since it was such a cold night knowing he wouldn't refuse. This man was a caffeine addict whose entire coffee supply I had removed earlier and so he had been unable to procure his usual flask for his night-time walk. He must be itching for it by now.

I think it was about halfway through his second cup that he realised something was amiss. If my dosage was correct, his vision should be getting blurry, his head hurting and his loss of consciousness should come any minute now.

A sudden gleam of understanding dawned in his dull, puzzled eyes and I basked in his fear dropping all pretences. This part was almost as fun as the main event. Unfortunately after the drugging came the nasty part. I disliked loud noises intensely and this required an utterly unmistakable one. Luckily I had a place where it would be muffled.

Carrying him to the warehouse, I left him in a crumpled heap as I double checked the area and then unlocked the rusting door. I crept inside and left my art tools down on a table beside the spread tarpaulin I had placed there a few days ago, then I returned. He was stirring. My smile was smug. Again. Perfect timing.

I placed him carefully in the centre of the tarp and methodically tied his limbs to a peg at each corner leaving him spread-eagled face up towards me. I removed his clothes and spared the weakly flickering bulb above me a brief glance of irritation. A moment later his eyes opened and blinked wildly. The once sapphire orbs were hazy and dulled under the influence of the drug but still retained a spark of awareness. Good. My research pegged this man as a fighter and I hate being wrong. He groaned and tried to move but couldn't. My Scout approved knots made sure of that. Slowly, so beautifully slowly, horrified realisation crept into his eyes and he turned to me begging and pleading. I simply smiled politely and raised a gun. Oh how I hated this part but it had to be done. His life was getting in the way of my art. I carefully aimed at his forehead. I wasn't cruel. I never prolonged any pain, I simply needed to create and he was the perfect canvas. His begging increased and I winced. He was getting loud. His eyes met mine and I gave him a slightly apologetic smile coupled with a shrug before pulling the trigger.

A single shot to the forehead. Perfect. Symmetrical. Beautiful.

I waited in silence listening for any footsteps and watching the blood drain through a hole in the sheet into the drains below. Seven minutes I lasted before the urge became too strong. A personal record. Turning to my kit I surveyed it critically and removed a thin silver scalpel. This was what I'd been waiting for. This is what made all the research worth it, what made enduring the stupidity of the rest of the world bearable. This was what I lived for. I never got tired of the thrill. Bringing the scalpel to kiss his flesh I made a single cut watching the red well up on my perfect, white canvas. Finally the hard part was over. Now I could lose myself in my art and perhaps if I was lucky, someone would finally see my brilliance.

Glimpsed Moments

by Doireann Ní Dhufaigh, aged 17

Water dripped slowly, pedantically. It created a syncopated rhythm. Its echo resonated, reverberated in the growing light. The branches of a dead tree were visible and the grey-white lustre brightened in the dawn. Close to a small rectangular window a spider was dangling from its web. It ascended and descended an invisible rope as it waited and plotted as the light illuminated the intricate strands of the elaborate architectural trap it had built.

Water dripped slowly, deliberately. He sat up in his cot; damp and shuddering from his nocturnal imaginings. He hadn't slept. He never slept anymore, too tired, too much of the hiddenness of the other world needed to fill the private moments of darkness. How could he rest? That was a luxury of the free. How he envied those who slept in the shade on their verandas. How he was jealous of those who withdrew into a feast of siestas or those who napped in the chairs that lined the labyrinthine alleyways and walkways of the city.

Water dripped slowly, rhythmically. He was never truly alone in all of this. The ghosts of the dead lingered around his stone-walled cell mingling with the smell of stale sweat and fear. The maniacal mutterings of the other inmates filled the silence. Their moaning and guttural prayers were a constant, as if they believed some divine, redemptive light would be shed upon them in this unrelenting darkness. Kalif sent his invocations to Allah, following the rituals of the bells and signals that sounded from the minarets and the domes that echoed from the town. His voice joined with the others who stretched out their prayer mats, those who sought forgiveness and fortune. Mapan prayed for forgetfulness while old Maia prayed for death. Kali's worn voice trembled as he begged Allah for solace, Suda's deep groans told of the pleasures that were denied him here and old Pandra's silence was more haunting than the sounds of the others. Silence was an enemy here, a corrosiveness that ate into everything.

Water dripped slowly, menacingly. He reached for his notebook and pencil on the cold bare floor and flipped it open. Inside, the pencil lines meandered on the page, scrawling eyes and arms and hands, and somehow they represented his friends and children. The forms on the page spoke to him as he struggled to remember the details. Did Amram have blue eyes? Had Mariam a mark on her left cheek or her right? He remembered them playing in the park, jumping hopscotch and riding swings as they flew momentarily through the air, squealing with delight as the swing got higher and higher. He struggled to recount his wife and yet he remembered her hazel brown eyes, dancing eyes. He recollected her small hands, the henna tattoos that told stories of woven flowers and magical gardens and princes and tales that seemed so exotic in this place. The guards told them not to dream and sometimes the memories of the outside world burned like a haunting.

Water dripped slowly, relentlessly. The sound of the hobnailed boots reverberated along the corridor. The guards were moving and the smell of cigarettes lingered. He could see their feet as they passed the cell door, shiny black leather. They dragged an inmate from his cell. The prisoners wore no shoes and the scratched and bloody soles told strange narratives in this place. They beat the bottoms of their feet and their screams pierced the corners of the building, vibrating through the air, frightening the birds and they wove their way into the dreams of the other inmates. Around him the sobs of the forgotten could be heard.

Water dripped slowly, evocatively. He remembered that he had been visiting his cousin Tariq in Kabul, the city of contrasts; a beautiful yet paranoid place. Driving through the streets in Tariq's jeep, the dust rose off the ground in twisting swirls. They sang in hoarse unison in that strange American tongue. They passed colourful stalls and the men were bartering in loud voices, reproachful voices that concealed the hiddenness and delight in their game of words. Approaching the bustling square they heard screams and the sudden wrenching sound of a gunshot. Soldiers in green, armed with steel rifles, yelling in harsh voices were everywhere. There was a checkpoint, hulking tanks rolled by leaving caterpillar tracks in their wake.

The water trickled and he remembered how Tariq swerved and cursed under his breath and then another shot rang out. Tariq was thrown back with the impact; blood spat from his head in sickening spurts and splashed all over his face. Chaos. Screams. Blurring confusion. Fear. There had been no time to take in what had just happened as he was pulled brusquely from the jeep. The soldiers roared in his blood and tear-drenched face, hissing words of anger and violence. His face seemed livid, like that of the grotesque gods he had read about as a boy. Another soldier brought something heavy down on his head, then nothingness and the empty womb of this dark cell.

The water stopped. His laboured breathing and throbbing head were what let him know he was in the moment that was real, and that it was not just another strange vision of his scrambled mind. Clutching his notebook, he rocked backwards and forwards. Too many days. Too many dreams. Too many painful moments when he recounted the places and the faces he loved.

Now all there was waiting, waiting for the guards to make their move. It was like a game; yes all this was a game. The figures he had drawn in charcoal huddled around him in ceremonious silence, his wife held him close as he sobbed and his children sat at his feet, sombre. The sounds from around withdrew into the dusk, caught in the dust that floated in the lines of light that filtered through. They would come soon ... too soon.

Water dripped slowly, pedantically. It created a syncopated rhythm. Its echo resonated, reverberated in the growing light. The branches of a dead tree were visible and the grey-white lustre brightened in the dawn. Close to a small rectangular window a spider was dangling from its web. It ascended and descended an invisible rope as it waited and plotted as the light illuminated the intricate strands of the elaborate architectural trap it had built...

Love the Life You Live

by Gráinne Hamill, aged 16

'One good thing about music, when it hits you, you feel no pain.'
– Bob Marley

Bob Marley plays in her ears as she walks towards her locker. Seeing heads turn, she doesn't bother reading their lips – knowing the words being thrown her way, 'Freak, fat, ugly.' She can feel the snigger's from all those that judged her the very first moment they saw her. She fumbles with the key to open her locker. Trying to erase her thoughts and letting the music overtake her soul.

Music gets her through her days; from the moment she wakes to the moment she falls asleep each night. There is a song out there for every emotion she ever feels. Music is there for her even when no one is. She doesn't feel alone when the music plays inside her ears, she feels like someone out there gets her, understands her, someone out there isn't judging her.

***

'You never know how strong you are – until being strong is your only choice' – Bob Marley

The razor is held between her sweaty fingers, as her heart race picks up – the same thought, gnawing at the back of her brain 'Do it, Do it, Do it' and that's when she screams, throwing the razor into the darkest corner of the room.

She can never press the razor to her skin – well that's a lie – She does press it to her skin, every single day, but she has yet to let it press so deep it hurts, it bleeds or it might even kill her.

She is afraid of death and that is what stops her every time, she's afraid of pain – emotionally and physically. Her heart aches each time she tries to smile. She is weak. And weak people like her don't get to have it easy.

But life is too precious to throw away, and she realizes in that moment that sometimes your only option is to be strong, one day it will all be easier.

***

'Some people feel the rain. Others just get wet.' – Bob Marley

The rain skims against the hard gravel, as she walks to her next class. She watches the students running to get away from the rain, and a light smile crosses her face as her eyes land on a boy with long brown dreads resting on his shoulders. His light blue eyes shine as he walks slowly to class. She can see it in his face as he lets the rain hit against him. He isn't just getting wet, he is feeling the rain.

She has always loved the rain, and watching someone else love it too; it brings light to dark parts of her heart. Some people out there really do appreciate the simple things in life, the things that don't cost a penny – the things that you don't have to search too much for. As the rain hits her skin, she finds herself thinking about that boy, thinking about how beautiful he was, how alike they must be.

***

'Herb is the healing of a nation, alcohol is the destruction.' – Bob Marley

She smells the smoke before she sees where it is coming from. She is sitting beneath an old oak tree around the corner of the school as she sits writing about her day so far. When she looks up that's when she sees him. The boy who had been walking in the rain the day before, not paying any attention to how other students were running to hide from it, he cared only about feeling it hit against his skin.

His eyes rest on hers and she quickly looks down at her notepad, a blush crossing her cheeks. She hears his footsteps approach her, her heart rate picked up.

'Want some?' She hears his deep Irish accent mutter, as she looks up into his beautiful eyes.

'Never tried weed before,' she mumbles, a small smile playing on her face.

'Weed is good for the system, much better than alcohol, promise!' He replies his face lighting up as she takes the joint from him.

***

'Who are you to judge the life I live? I know I'm not perfect – and I don't live to be – but before you start pointing fingers... make sure your hands are clean!' – Bob Marley

She sat at the back of the class – the bell ringing out as she packed up her stuff – not bothering a soul. A girl walking by banged into her; but as the girl turned to say sorry, her face quickly changed a look of realisation spread over her. An evil smile spread across her face as she laughed, turning to walk away.

'What's your problem?' She found the words had left her lips before she could stop them.

'Excuse me?' the girl asked, turning in shock. She never spoke, and when she did, it wasn't to question another on why they always treated her badly.

A hush descended on the room and she could feel eyes now upon her. She wished she had kept her mouth shut, but now she had started she had to finish.

'Who said you had the right to judge me? All of you think you're something special because you fit within society, but you know something I'm ten times the person you are.' She spat, as she scanned the room, glaring into the eyes of those she had avoided until now.

***

'The greatness of a man is not in how much wealth he acquires, but in his integrity and his ability to affect those around him positively' – Bob Marley

She stood in the art room, painting a picture. It was an image that had just come to her mind that morning. Two figures, one female, the other male; stood in a black forest, darkness

116

surrounded them, yet they looked like angels. A torchlight in the dark, the good within the evil.

She felt a hand touch her back, her heart rate raced as she spun around the paintbrush held out as if it were going to protect her against any evil. She heard his laugh her heart rate slowed, her arm coming to rest calmly by her side.

'You okay?' he laughed, as his eyes rested on her painting, studying it.

'Um, fine, what about you?' she awkwardly turned towards her painting, dipping her paintbrush in the paint, and shading some more.

His hand came to rest upon hers, and she turned her head – looking into his beautiful blue eyes, as he shook his head and a smile came to his face, making his eyes shine bright.

'It's perfect don't do anything else to it,' his voice making her nerves calm, and she nodded yet she was confused as to why she had listened to him.

It made her smile. Crazy; how short of a time you could know someone, how little you could know about them, yet they could make you feel better than anyone had made you feel in years.

***

'Overcome the devils with a thing called love.' – Bob Marley

Even though the devils overtook her soul each night as she fell asleep, something had changed inside her, something beyond explanation. He was constantly on her mind. His blue eyes were engraved in her memory; she could feel his hands touch her lightly – as if she were breakable. Even though she hardly ever spoke to him, she fell asleep thinking up conversations that they'd have between each other the following day – in her mind at least.

Some might not believe in love, but she was starting to become one of those who did believe in that four-letter word.

***

'You can fool some people sometimes but you can't fool all the people all the time' – Bob Marley

'You can act like you're tough, you can fool others, but I can see it in your eyes every time you smile – that you are close to tears, close to breaking,' he mumbled as she sat on her bed, he made his way closer to her, her breath catching in her throat.

'Okay, okay that's enough. We can quit with the play, it's boring me,' she smiled, it was a weak smile – hoping to get away from the pain she could feel in her heart, from the thought of him knowing how messed up she was deep down.

He placed his body down on the bottom of the bed, just by her feet.

'You know you can talk to me right? You know I get you. I see you in ways most of the fools in this world don't?' He expressed, his lips turning up into a warm smile; a reassuring smile, a smile that said 'I'm here' no matter what.

She understood in that moment she could fool most people, but she couldn't fool him.

***

'To love is to risk, not being loved in return. To hope is to risk pain. To try is to risk failure, but risk must be taken because the greatest hazard in my life is to risk nothing.' – Bob Marley

She walks towards him; he is standing beneath the tree where she smoked her first joint. His eyes come up to meet hers, and he smiles at her, a smile she returns.

Without saying anything, she quickly grabs his face lightly between her two small hands. She places a small kiss on his lips before pulling away, looking into his eyes to make sure it's okay, and before she knows it they are passionately kissing, exploring each other.

The risk she has taken has paid off, and for once she feels accepted and not denied.

All the things she has dreamt up in her mind were suddenly coming through. The way he held her close like he wanted her, but far enough apart for her to feel like she was also could fly free at any moment – the way his lips met hers; soft yet hard enough for it to be full of passion.

***

'Just because you are happy it does not mean that the day is perfect but that you have looked beyond its imperfections' – Bob Marley

She awakes with a smile on her face, her eyes looking like another dark cloud has left them, and even though there are many more beneath them she feels like one weight has been lifted from her shoulders today.

Life is not perfect, and she has come to realise that over the last couple of months, but in life we all have a story to create and you can't always let the negative things rule your life. Nothing and no one is perfect, but sometimes you must live life to its fullest, looking past the imperfections.

We must see each day as a fresh start – we must grab hold of the chances in which are offered to us – we must be positive.

She has learnt so much from one boy that's life isn't perfect, but who lives each day knowing that if he just smiles, he may change another person's day. That lives each moment like it is his last.

How you live your life – well it's up to you. But we all get to make our own destiny, while we should also never forget our past. Our past makes us, but does not own us. Our destiny is who we will be, but it is never written in stone what we should be, should do.

She walks to the mirror and instead of seeing someone that is ugly, overweight, freaky. She sees a beautiful girl with all the best years of her life still to come. She smiles and for once she looks forward to the day ahead of her.

... the dust and seep of the city ...

by Doireann Ní Dhufaigh, aged 17

A descriptive essay about twenty-four hours in the life of a town or city.

There was a baffled percussive beat to the air like a heart, beating
... beating ... beating. A dull, gauzy-grey chemical sky enveloped
the morning. Weak slivers of light filtered through the clouds and
the odour of old rancid blood from the slaughterhouses along the
river permeated the air on humid days. He sat alone, amongst the
leaping rooftops of the city, a bleak place full of confusion, hope
and Gothic architecture.

The heart beat on, rhythmically. He savoured the pool of
silence that was the city, his city, soon to be interrupted by the
squabbling of the Jorches, their domestic dramas providing a black
comedy for Rezi's twisted sense of humour. He had never spoken
to them and had no wish to do so. This was how he thought of
people now: they were souls, they were transient spirits, a face in
the window of a passing car, runny with reflected light, or a long
street with a shovel jutting from a snowbank, no one in sight.

The heart beat on, repetitively. He stood up and stretched,
spilling his coffee as he did so. He hadn't slept, he never slept
anymore. Too tired, too much of the hiddenness from other
worlds needed to fill the private moments of darkness. He traipsed
inside his apartment, the interior a myriad of torn canvasses,
books, copies and unwashed plates. He showered, dressed and
took upon himself the task of shaving two months' worth of facial
hair, now an obnoxious unruly barb. The bathroom mirror, almost
cruel in its all-revealing honesty reflected his image, his milky eyes,
blood-shot and ringed, surveyed this parody of a man. No vestige
of colour could be seen in his face, his aquiline nose, slightly
crooked, told violent narratives. Steam rose from the sink in
twisting swirls, mercifully clouding the vision.

The heart beat on, pedantically. In snowfall, the city looked
ghosted over. As the winter deepened, Rezi's days became toned

with sadness and other, unspeakable things. He made his way towards Saul Strasse to the gallery where he had spent the last three days. He wove through the labyrinthine alleyways and walkways where you could still hear the steps of the dead at night sometimes. Half the world rushed by around him, he was indifferent to their haste though. He had long since left behind him any urgency or fastidious time-keeping pertaining to his character, such attention to insignificant detail had no place in this private chaos. In his pocket he fingered the remnants of what had once imprisoned him, divided the city's people like mice. He felt like David in that biblical horror story, having conquered the monstrous leviathan.

The heart beat on, relentlessly. He knew there was someone else it the room. There was no outright noise, just an intimation behind him, a faint displacement of air. He'd been alone for a time, seated on a bench in the middle of the gallery with the paintings set around him, a cycle of fifteen canvasses, and this was how it felt to him, that he was sitting, as a person does, in a mortuary chapel, keeping watch over the body of a relative or a friend.

The heart beat on, deliberately. He was looking at Olysa now, head and upper body, her neck rope-scorched though he did not know what kind of implement had been used in the hanging. He heard the other person come towards the bench, a man's heavy shuffling stride, and he got up and went to stand before the picture of Olysa, one of three related images. Olysa is dead in each, lying on the floor of her cell, head in profile. The canvasses varied in size, the woman's reality, the head, the neck, the rope burn, the hair. The facial features were painted picture to picture in nuances of obscurity and pall, a detail clearer here than there, a slurred mouth in one painting appearing almost natural elsewhere, all of it unsystematic. 'Why do you think she did it this way?' He did not turn to look at him as he continued, 'so shadowy, no colour'. 'I don't know', he replied tersely and turned to the next set of images called 'Transience'.

The heart beat on, disjointedly. These were a sequence of paintings based on a young man, Hulbert Braun 'I'm trying to understand what happened to them', Rezi said. 'They committed suicide, or the state killed them', he said. 'The state', then he said it again, deep-voiced, in a tone of melodramatic menace, trying out a line reading that might be more suitable. He wanted to feel annoyed but felt instead a vague chagrin. It wasn't like him to use this term, 'the state.' In the iron-clad context of supreme public power, this was not his vocabulary. The two paintings of Braun, making to leap over the wall were the same size, but addressed the subject somewhat differently. And this is what he did now, he concentrated on the differences. Braun's flailing limbs, his shirt, his pupils dilated wildly, his mouth turned downwards in an almost canine grimace. The disparity, or uncertainty.

The heart beat on, wearily. 'A pact, they were terrorists weren't they? When they're not killing other people there killing themselves', the man said. Rezi was looking at Braun, first one painting, then the other, then back again. 'I don't know, that's worse in a way, it's so much sadder, there's so much sadness in these paintings' 'There's one where he's smiling'. This was Olysa in 'Proclamation 1'. 'I don't know if that's a smile, it could be a smile', Rezi muttered. 'It's the clearest image in the room, maybe the whole museum. I think she's smiling', the man retorted. He turned to look at Hulbert across the gallery and saw the man on the bench, half turned his way, wearing a suit with tie unknotted, going prematurely bald.

Rezi only glimpsed at him, he was staring at him but Rezi looked past him to the painting of Olysa, in a prison smock, standing against a wall and smiling most likely, yes, in the middle picture. Three pictures of Olysa smiling, smiling and probably not smiling. 'You need special training to look at these paintings. I can't tell the figures apart' 'Yes you can,' Rezi said, 'Look, you have to look,' he heard a note of slight reprimand in his voice. He went to the far wall to look at the painting of Hulbert's modest apartment, with tall book shelves covering half the canvas and a dark shape, wraithlike, that may have been a coat on a hanger.

The heart beat on, metrically. 'She died last year you know, only a month after the wall came down', said the man behind him, 'She wasn't particularly popular when she was alive, then some curators found these and the leeches decided to make some money out of her, put a retrospective together.' The heart beat on, meticulously. Two women entered the gallery, followed by a man with a cane, all three stood beside the explanatory material, reading. The painting of the coffins had something else that wasn't easy to find, he had not found it until the second day, and it was striking once he'd found it and it was inescapable now.

An object at the top of the painting – just left of centre, a tree perhaps in the rough shape of a cross. He went closer to the painting, hearing the man with the cane move towards the opposite wall. He knew that these paintings were based on photographs but he hadn't seen them and didn't know whether there was a bare tree, a dead tree beyond the cemetery in one of the photos. A paltry thing that consisted of a spindly trunk with a single branch remaining, or two branches forming a transverse piece near the top of the trunk. 'Tell me what you see, honestly, I wanna know'. A group entered, led by a guide, and he turned for a moment, watching them collect at the first painting in the cycle. The portrait of Olysa as a much younger woman, a girl really, distant and wistful, her hand and face half floating in the sombre dark around her.

The heart beat on, meticulously. 'I think I feel helpless', Rezi said softly. 'These paintings make me think how helpless a person can be.' He winced slightly, recalling unwanted memories. Images of her mutilated figure endlessly nagged at his subconscious. The black shower of bullets that rained death on her seared into his imagination – impregnably. Blue denim spattered with blood. 'Is that why you're here three days straight? To feel helpless?'

The heart stopped. It was a cross, he saw it as a cross, and it made him feel, right or wrong, that there was an element of forgiveness in the picture that Hulbert and Olysa, terrorists, radicals, were not beyond forgiveness. But he did not point out the cross to the man standing next to him. That was not what he wanted, a discussion on the subject. He didn't think he was imagining a cross, seeing a cross in some free strokes of paint, but he didn't want to hear someone raise elementary doubts.

At closing time he left the gallery, the receptionist bid him goodnight and he returned the sentiment, smiling weakly at her.

'Are You Alright?'

by Alana Mahon O'Neill, aged 16

He sat, curled into a ball again, as he always did. He could feel the needles leaving his rigid shoulders, moving down his body slowly until all he could feel was the prickling in his toes.

No matter what, it was still there. It was the feeling before a cramp came, an omniscient presence. As soon as he pressed his fingers towards the ground trying to stand, his hands flared. He couldn't bear to look at his fingers, which were certainly longer than usual. The prickles of stabbing pain, like internal hot blistering needles lodged beneath his skin were excruciatingly painful. If it were possible if he could see into his bones, he could witness the interwoven networks constructing and interlacing themselves, growing and stretching his skin outwards turning the blue, greyer and greyer until it looked grotesquely white.

Bursts of blood came to the surface; they burned as they touched the outer skin of his hands and inflamed as he brushed his elongated limb like fingers together. He could see the small limps travelling leisurely across the contortions and slither down his wrists. He could feel his circulation slowing down and it became hard, if near impossible, to breathe.

A huge heavy feeling was left in his chest – old air.

He let out the poison and his empty chest was left with nothing. His mind cleared slightly, yet he still felt stifled despite the fact he no longer need huge intakes of breath. He breathed very slowly, he could barely see his chest rising and falling. Air was expelled sluggishly from his warped frame. He didn't know how he could do it, how exactly it was controlled anyway, but he concentrated on the heat, the placid, pale knives as fingers that were attached to his hands. That crackling sensation again.

He fought the urge to start screaming. The pain of the bones returning into place – the delicate feeling of the stretching, lining and the bones become one again.

It was unbearable.

The lumps of moving blood flattened and the icy tone transitioning into a slightly darker grey. His face was wet. He thought he was crying again but as he flexed his still burning fingers to wipe his eyes, the salty substance returning was shrill, red and metallic-scented. They were bleeding.

He scrambled to his feet quickly, he made towards the sink. He was suddenly blinded by scarlet images he hadn't noticed before. It was as if the ground beneath him suddenly vanished as he fell towards the basin. He twisted the funnel hurriedly and collected freezing water in his hands before agitatedly throwing it into his choked vision. It took him a few seconds to comprehend that the water was indeed freezing. He always felt so cold that being splashed in the face with some was hardly bothering. However, as they hit his eyes, there came a burning sensation again.

He stopped, gathering himself together.

As he blinked a few more times, he could see clearly again. For some reason, his eyesight was perfect; he could make out every individual speck of dirt on the basin. His grey hands clutched fast on the sides.

Breath has returned to normal.

He corrected himself.

My breathing has returned to normal. This is I, this is me.

He lightly bit his tongue; light blood tasted in his mouth born from the cut that refused to heal. This didn't bother him as much as when his eyes were bleeding. He lazily lifted his hands and ran his hands through his hair. He hated the sight of his reflection; it always gave the impression that there was another person there with him, judging him. It alarmed him at first; he grew angry then, it was only him.

'I hate you.' His plain voice echoed coldly throughout the room. It felt like someone else speaking, as if he had never heard his own voice before. Even now he still didn't like it, it was like a stranger's opinion only reaffirming his own.

Felt better.

I'm feeling better.

He had grey skin and large sunken eyes, with flakes of blood around them like sleep. He was filthy and his hair looked greasy. Through his open mouth he could see the throbbing gash on his tongue and the blood on his incisors and canines. He felt as if he had been chewing his fingers, they hurt so much.

'I'm going to kill you...'

He feverishly slammed his fist against the mirror until the vermin in the mirror shattered into cobwebs in the frame. He could still make out the large sunken eyes, the blood. He pushed a fragment of glass deeper into the palm of his hand, yet he could already start to feel his skin rapidly heal over the foreign object. He wrenched it out and threw it to the floor. The small pieces that remained in his palm popped out and fell to the blood with a light tinkle. He shuffled uncomfortably, his feet crunching on glass.

He felt a flicker of something deep within his chest, it wasn't pain or anger.

His mouth twitched.

A knock sounded on the door.

'Pet, are you alright? You've been in there so long!'

His mother stood on the other side, unaware of what was happening to him. What he was becoming.

'Yes, I'm alright.' He lied; he reached across to the shower turning on the hot water to have a shower. He shivered in the cold despite the searing remains of the needles still stinging his wrists.

He couldn't tell anyone what was happening.

To Catch What Cannot Be Caught

by Annie Brown, aged 14

We walked through the dark streets, guided only by each other and the street lamps. Our fingers interwoven, we fell towards the tall metal gates of the playground. The town playground was less a place for the children, more a place where the teenagers of the town gathered. It was like a meeting point, if you got separated from the group, you'd be sure to find someone in the playground. The gates were locked and there was no way in, so we sat on the ground and tried to come up with a plan to get ourselves into the park unnoticed. The ground was damp, and made my bare legs cold and the back of my skirt wet. My feet hurt from wearing a pair of stupidly high heels all night so I kicked them off and held them on my lap as we brainstormed.

Eventually we decided to climb over the high railings, which went well until I landed face-first in a bed of shrubbery, which sort of sent my dignity (well, what was left of it) out the window. I got up, my head spinning, and straightened myself out. He jumped off the railing and landed lightly on his feet, which made me feel like even more of an idiot, then took my hand as we ran down the hill. We ran, our feet moving of their own accord, until eventually our feet couldn't take us anymore and they went from under us. We fell, and rolled down the slope, collapsing in a heap of giggles at the bottom. We lay there for a while, looking up at the giant moon, its pale glistening light making his green eyes sparkle under his fringe. Whatever we were drinking made everything a little bit prettier: the leaves were greener, the grass was softer, and the stars were brighter. It was cold, but we were close enough that I could feel his body heat against me. The moon shone so brightly and beautifully, I wanted some of it for my own so that I could always remember that night. I never wanted to forget that night – I had never realised how fun it was to lie in a drunken heap under the stars.

'Let's try catching the moon.' I whispered to him, my lips brushing his ear.

We got up and stumbled towards the swings, where we got up and pumped our legs as we went higher and higher, but not high enough. Our arms flailed, trying to reach the moon. He jumped off his swing, but I kept going, willing myself to get a little bit higher to try and get even the tiniest piece of the moon. He ran behind me, and started pushing me up, up, up. With my legs working harder than ever before, and him pushing me with all his might, we thought that maybe we might just manage it... but it was just the cheap contraband talking.

We let the swing slow down and when I got off, we lay on the ground again. I could feel his warmth against my side, his chest rising and falling with every breath he took. The swings creaked as I let my breathing match to his, so we were in sync when he took my hand.

'We could try jumping?' he suggested.

'We won't get up high enough to reach it,' I explained, frowning.

He sighed and sat up, still holding my hand.

'Then we have only one choice...' he began. I sat up next to him and looked at him questionably, my eyebrows raised. I could smell drink and cigarettes off him, but I didn't care. His eyes looked bright and clear under his brown hair, and he leaned in to me and whispered: 'Sing, sing to the moon'. His voice was distorted with drunkenness, and I knew mine was too as I tried to laugh and it came out as a half-giggle, half-hiccup.

'That's the most ridiculous thing I've ever heard,' I laughed.

'It's our only hope!' he announced dramatically, standing up and spreading his arms wide. 'We've got no other choice!'

'What will we sing?' I hiccupped again, laughing still.

'Twinkle, Twinkle!' he yelled. 'Mary Had a Little Lamb!'

We laughed and laughed, falling up and down the deserted pathways in the park, until we could see the sunlight rising over the tops of the trees. We both knew that our night was ending, that we'd soon have to face the consequences of enraged parents and pounding headaches and vowing never to do that again so long as we live.

As we heard somebody open the creaky metal gates, we knew it was time to go. He looked down at me, his eyes not so bright and clear anymore, and he kissed me. He tasted like stale, illegally obtained beer, but I guessed I did too so I didn't say anything. He kissed me softly until we heard a voice yelling at us.

'Hey, how did you get in here?! The gates weren't open since yesterday!'

He broke away, gave me a drunken smile and took off running. He ran the opposite way to the voice that was calling to us, making his getaway.

'What are you doing here?' the voice asked, coming closer to me.

'I was just leaving.' I slurred, turning and walking away. It was a night to remember, I knew that much. I learned a lot of things from that night. I learned that he was a mistake for one, because I never saw him again. I learned that there were a lot of things I could catch, but sometimes certain things just weren't meant to be caught.

www.ingramcontent.com/pod-product-compliance
Lightning Source LLC
Chambersburg PA
CBHW060125260626
47160CB00005B/2021